"Would you really ⟨ **were doing this my way?"**

She turned back to look at him.

Reese was moving toward her, then stopped in his tracks. "No."

She let herself relax a little.

"But we are going to do this the safest way possible. And that's for us to work together. Not as backup, but as a team. Okay?"

He was asking her opinion, but she didn't fool herself into thinking she had a choice. The decision had been made. It was written all over his face. "You're stubborn."

"And that's a bad quality?" A ghost of a smile played on his lips. "Not anything like you, is it?"

She bit back a grin. Okay, so she also had a stubborn streak. Point taken.

"I can handle this mission," she said, not sure if she was trying to convince him or herself.

He held her gaze. "Yes, you can. But I'll be right there with you all the same. Never forget that."

DANA MARTON

MY BODYGUARD

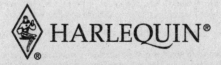

HARLEQUIN®

TORONTO • NEW YORK • LONDON
AMSTERDAM • PARIS • SYDNEY • HAMBURG
STOCKHOLM • ATHENS • TOKYO • MILAN • MADRID
PRAGUE • WARSAW • BUDAPEST • AUCKLAND

With many thanks to Allison Lyons, Maggie Scillia and Monica Reider for all their support and generous help.

ISBN-13: 978-0-373-69274-3
ISBN-10:   0-373-69274-9

MY BODYGUARD

Copyright © 2007 by Dana Marton

ABOUT THE AUTHOR

Author Dana Marton lives near Wilmington, Delaware. She has been an avid reader since childhood and has a master's degree in writing popular fiction. When not writing, she can be found either in her garden or her home library. For more information on the author and her other novels, please visit her Web site at www.danamarton.com.

She would love to hear from her readers via e-mail: DanaMarton@yahoo.com.

Books by Dana Marton

HARLEQUIN INTRIGUE
  821—SECRET SOLDIER
  859—THE SHEIK'S SAFETY
  875—CAMOUFLAGE HEART
  902—ROGUE SOLDIER
  917—PROTECTIVE MEASURES
  933—BRIDAL OP
  962—UNDERCOVER SHEIK
  985—SECRET CONTRACT*
  991—IRONCLAD COVER*
1007—MY BODYGUARD*

*Mission: Redemption

CAST OF CHARACTERS

Samantha Hanley—Sam ran away from home at an early age and spent years on the streets before ending up in prison. Now that she's been recruited for a dangerous mission, will she be able to face down her demons and survive?

Reese Moretti—A professional bodyguard who agrees to go undercover to protect Sam. He thought the information the FBI is willing to give him in exchange was the most important thing in his life…until he met Sam.

Brant Law—FBI agent in charge of Samantha and her three teammates.

Nick Tarasov—Member of the Special Designation Defense Unit. He trained the women for the mission at Quantico, Virginia.

David Moretti—The women's legal advisor.

Carly Jones, Gina Torno and Anita Caballo—The other three members of Samantha's team.

Tsernyakov—Illegal weapons trader and among the five most wanted criminals in the world.

Philippe Cavanaugh—An international businessman who is up to his neck in dirty dealings. His connection to Tsernyakov links him to a pending terrorist attack.

Roberto—One of Philippe's men who has his own designs on Sam.

Prologue

Quantico, Virginia

FBI agent Brant Law pointed to the screen that showed the dark outline of a man's profile. "Your target is someone who has managed to elude law enforcement for the last twenty years. He has no known picture. We haven't been able to narrow his location to as much as a country. We don't know his first name, or exactly how old he is."

David Moretti, the team's gorgeous lawyer, and Nick Tarasov, the commando guy who had seen to the four women's training at Quantico, flanked him on either side.

Samantha Hanley watched the men with distrust, much like the three other women sitting around her.

In exchange for signing up for a top-secret mission, they were let out of Brighton Federal

Correctional Institute. If they succeeded, their sentences would be canceled and their records cleared. She didn't expect much to come of it—her luck didn't usually work that way—but she'd been willing to take the risk.

Got her out of that cell, didn't it?

"So what do you know?" Gina Torno, the ex-cop who'd slipped and killed a man, spoke up.

"We know him as Tsernyakov. But we're not sure if that's his real name. He is one of the biggest illegal-weapons dealers in the world. We suspect he might have had some position in the old communist government in the USSR, might have been in the military—his access to large amounts of decommissioned weaponry points that way. He has 'ears' in every branch of law enforcement of just about every country. He has unlimited access to money. He is ruthless. If he thinks someone crossed him, he doesn't wait for proof. He kills on first suspicion."

"You want us to do what? Take him out?" Gina asked.

The air stuck in Sam's lungs, the question making her realize what a small-timer, a thief that's all, she was compared to some of the other women.

But Law said, "Getting a location on him would be enough."

And she let herself relax a little.

The questions and answers flew back and forth.

"Your cover will be a consulting company that facilitates entrepreneurs in setting up small businesses. Miss Caballo will handle accounting, Miss Jones will do IT, Miss Torno will take care of security, including background checks on employees and Miss Hanley is the support person for the team."

"I'm the freakin' secretary? No way." So what if she'd come from the streets? It didn't mean the rest were better.

"You're an undercover agent in a top-secret operation." Law appeared sincere.

Didn't sound *that* horrid when he put it like that. If she didn't like how things unfolded, she could always take off. They would never find her. She was good at running.

Law showed them another slide, mission statement and other information on their made-up company.

"What else do you want us to do? A start-up consulting outfit isn't going to attract much attention from the type Tsernyakov would hang with," Gina challenged him again.

"Correct. Savall, Ltd. is your cover. What you'll really be involved in is money laundering."

"Are you asking us to engage in illegal activities?" Anita looked as stunned and morally outraged as a Girl Scout asked to kick puppies. A good actress, that one.

"You need to move in the same circles Tsernyakov's associates move in. You're authorized by the FBI and CIA to use any means necessary to get close to the man."

Sam tugged at the silver rings in her eyebrow.

"This is not gonna come back to bite us, no matter what?" Gina asked.

"Correct."

"You need us, people with authentic backgrounds instead of existing agents, because if we get lucky enough to catch this guy's attention he'll have us checked out and he knows people in the right places." Gina kept pushing.

"Yes."

"I'm guessing something like this would be a last-ditch effort. You tried before with your own men and didn't succeed. Did he have them killed?" Gina shot back again.

"We lost a number of operatives." Law moved on to the next slide, an explanation on what Savall, Ltd. did and the business in general.

"Miss Caballo was convicted for the embezzlement of nearly four million dollars that was never recovered. Your operations will imply that she had that money safely stashed away, met up with the rest of you in prison and decided to start a company that would grow her nest egg outside the United States."

Way to go. Sam grinned at Anita, who was looking at Law with a tight-lipped expression.

"So what's going to keep us from taking off once you cut us loose?"

Gina's question claimed Sam's full attention. *This* she wanted to hear.

"You'll be under constant surveillance. For your own safety." Law indicated Tarasov.

Commando-guy was going to babysit? Well, that was his burden. He was good, but he hadn't seen Sam in action yet. She had evaded drunks and druggies and gangs and cops for too many years on the street to be held down by anyone.

"Any questions about this part?" Law asked.

Anita raised her hand. *Raised her hand.* Like, where were they, in middle school? She had to be faking all that ladylike respect for authority. Anyone who'd made off with four million couldn't really be like that. "Has anyone managed to get close to this man and come back alive?"

The FBI agent looked at Moretti and Tarasov before addressing the women. "None so far," he said.

Sam stared into the sudden silence in the room.

Either this was a chance to start over, or the biggest mistake she'd ever made in her life. And yet she was desperate to give it a try. Because she did want to start over. She was scared to death of always being thought of as a former street kid turned petty criminal. Would society ever let her climb out of that box?

And the most terrifying question of all: what if they did and she wasn't capable?

Chapter One

Georgetown, Grand Cayman Island,
three months later

"I don't think it's a good idea," Sam Hanley said, standing by her desk in the middle of Savall, Ltd.'s office on Grand Cayman Island with David, Anita, Gina and Carly around her. "I don't mind going alone."

Going undercover at a week-long beach party at the closely guarded compound of a known criminal sounded scary, sure, but she was forever falling over her own feet near David Moretti and his mile-wide charisma. If she slipped at Cavanaugh's, she could mess up everything. It would be better to go alone and be able to focus.

"Let's keep in mind that David is an attorney and has no training for a situation like this," Brant Law said over the speaker. "Cavanaugh is the only link to Tsernyakov that we've been able to turn up. There is no margin for error."

He was patched in via phone, along with Nick Tarasov. Now that they were getting close to their target, the men had stepped back and were careful not to show themselves in the company of the four women. No sense arousing any suspicions and risk blowing their cover.

"David's not the rough-and-tough type," Nick said. "No offense."

"None taken. I'm smooth. That's what I do." David smiled, clearly at ease with who he was and wasn't, a trait Sam envied.

"Since Cavanaugh thinks David is your boyfriend, you two better be convincing." Gina gave Sam an amused glance.

Hey, it could happen. In an alternate universe. Sam flashed back a defensive look, knowing David was miles out of her league.

Though Cavanaugh wasn't supposed to meet David at all, they had run into him the day before and introductions had been unavoidable. So they'd been nervous, acting frazzled, and the man had thought they'd been coming from a lunchtime tryst, assuming they were romantically linked. And they hadn't corrected him, because they had no better explanation handy.

Dark hair, sharp gray eyes, great smile—David

had style, big-time, and he carried himself like a movie star, plenty of sex appeal rounding out the picture. He wore a dark suit despite the heat, some light wonder of silk. A man like him wouldn't have given her the time of day under normal circumstances. Not that it mattered much. David was off-limits anyway. He had some supermodel wife and not the brainless kind, either, one of the better-known ones, co-owner of some posh NYC restaurant—a depressing piece of information she'd overheard from Brant Law.

You shouldn't ever feel inferior, not to anyone. Sam drew herself tall. Anita had told her that. Maybe someday she would start to believe it.

Sick as it sounded, David's inaccessibility was probably part of her attraction. She could safely have a crush on the man without having to fear that it would ever come to anything. She didn't, at heart, want a relationship—wasn't ready, wasn't sure she ever would be. But it was a nice fantasy to think that she was capable.

"I think Cavanaugh likes you. I've seen him staring at you before. And he always asks about you when I call," Anita said.

"Yeah, right." Sam rolled her eyes as she shrugged off the suggestion.

"So we may assume that Cavanaugh invited

Sam because he has a special interest in her?"
David looked at Sam more carefully.

Her heart fluttered.

"He sure didn't invite the rest of us," Gina bit
back.

"Because you weren't there." Sam gave her the
duh look. David had been bringing legal papers to
the island for Anita to sign, since her name had
been cleared. He ran into Sam in the lobby and
they came up together, bumped into Cavanaugh,
who was coming from a meeting with Anita. The
suave Frenchman was one of Tsernyakov's right-
hand men, their biggest break in the case so far.
They chatted for a few minutes, and the next thing
she knew, they were both invited to the man's
beach party.

"I still cannot comprehend why I was asked
to participate along with Samantha." David
glanced around.

"Sam," she corrected. She hated Samantha.
Buck had called her that. She didn't want to think
about Buck, now or as long as she lived.

David Moretti made that easy. She couldn't
think whatsoever when he was around.

"Maybe he wants to check out the competition,"
Gina supplied the answer to his question. "Maybe
he thought Sam wouldn't go without you."

"He definitely thinks we're together. He called

him *my David* when he invited him." Sam felt her face flush. Gina was probably right. Her proximity to David had made her nervous. And they *had* been surprised by Cavanaugh, who wasn't supposed to be in the office that day. He'd been in the neighborhood and dropped in to iron out some details on a deal with Anita.

"Anyway," Gina said, "I think the two of you going together is a good idea. It'll hold Cavanaugh back a little. If he was all over Sam, she couldn't get any substantial recon done."

"I've never discharged a weapon in my life." David brought up his hands in a defensive gesture. "What would I be required to do?"

"You're not going there for a shoot-out." Gina clicked her tongue with impatience. "But just in case anything goes wrong, you can learn. They all did." She gestured toward Anita, Carly and Sam.

"By the day after tomorrow?" Nick asked over the phone.

"The answer is no," Brant emphasized. "Someone who is not ready for this would only become a liability. The invitation is a huge step forward. Let's not mess it up. It would have taken us weeks to set up some kind of covert entry, figuring out security, working blind. Sam will be allowed in and shown around, and given free rein of the grounds."

"No pressure." Sam tried to joke off the weight she was starting to feel.

"I want to go in," Nick suggested, not for the first time.

"You can't." Brant shot him down again. "Neither of us can show. We have ties to law enforcement that go back too far. If he does any kind of check at all, we'll pop up and the mission is over before we get within sniffing distance of Tsernyakov."

There was a moment of silence then Brant spoke again. "Okay, David. How about your brother?"

Sam looked at him. He had a brother?

"I find it highly improbable that Reese would consent to participate." He shook his head.

"I'll just say David couldn't make it and go alone." Sam came to his defense. "A switch wouldn't work, anyway, unless they're twins. Cavanaugh had a pretty good look at him."

David flashed her one of his mind-melting smiles as he nodded. "No worries there."

Her eyes went wide. David Moretti had a twin. Two of him. Like one wasn't overwhelming enough.

"So this brother of yours, he's the rough-and-tough type?" Gina asked. "If he's going with Sam, he'd better be able to provide protection."

"He is a professional bodyguard," Brant cut in. "He's somewhat of a wild card from what I understand."

David didn't respond. His eyes were becoming somber, although the ever-present smile never faltered on his face.

"Sounds like a good alternative," Anita said with caution. "I think it would be smart for Sam not to go alone."

She didn't mean it disparagingly, as if Sam wasn't capable. Anita was simply the mothering type. She couldn't help being concerned about others' safety. It no longer bothered Sam. God knew, she had a serious deficiency when it came to being mothered. Still, she didn't want to look as if she were scared of the mission, especially not in front of the others. She wasn't ready to let them see any of the chinks in her armor. You showed weakness and the world steamrolled right on over you. It was a lesson she had learned well on the street.

"It's a beach party. I'll get a tan, check out the house, draw some blueprints, eavesdrop if I can. What can go wrong?" She shrugged as if her scalp weren't tingling from nerves. "I *can* do it." She didn't feel nearly as sure as she sounded, but what was the alternative? Have the others figure out what a screwup she was, kick her off the team and send her back to the can?

"You can if you need to," Brant said, apparently buying her bravado. "But it looks like we are getting a chance to put in a second man. It's a freebie, a bonus. He could watch your back. You could go further, get more information."

"I shouldn't have introduced David by his real name." Sam shook her head. She'd been kicking herself for that ever since. But who could think standing next to David Moretti?

"That was probably a good move actually," Brant said. "Cavanaugh will have him investigated prior to the party. He wouldn't let a complete stranger inside his compound. If he caught us in a lie, it would jeopardize the whole operation."

A moment of silence passed, then Carly turned to David. "You think your brother could handle this?"

"He could, but he won't. It's not what he does. He escorts businessmen in politically unstable areas. He navigates the hot spots, retrieves kidnap victims, that kind of thing." He hesitated.

"And?" Brant was asking. "This is not about preferences." He paused for a moment. "I just received the latest report an hour ago, didn't want to mention it until I had a chance for another look and a more careful analysis, but there is so much bustle in terrorist circles, the lines are glowing. Monies are moving, human resources are being re-shuffled. We've never seen this much activity." He paused again. "Not even before 9/11."

"Something major is about to go down," Nick picked up where Brant had left off. "Since Tsernyakov rules the illegal-weapons market, chances are he's in on it. If we can get to him, we might be able to stop whatever is about to happen."

And Cavanaugh was their only link to Tsernyakov. Cavanaugh, who had just invited her to spend a week at his house. Everything rode on her. Odd doubts surfaced, one after the other. What if she wasn't equal to the task?

At the beginning, she had taken the deal without much thought because it got her out of prison, and to show them all that she wasn't scared of anything. But as she'd gotten to know the others over the past months, it was becoming more and more important not to let them down. She wanted to get Tsernyakov, for the team, and for herself, too, to prove that she could do something right for once.

"So, David, how about Reese?" Brant asked. "Without telling him everything, of course. Strictly on a need-to-know basis."

"I'll attempt to persuade him. However, the last time I requested a favor from him it turned out rather unfavorably. He was guarding one of my clients prior to court testimony and she allegedly shot him in the back. I don't believe I can convince him to discard whatever he's working on to come and bail me out again."

"What's a bullet in the back between brothers?" Gina joked.

David shook his head. "His exact words were, *Never again. You don't even have to ask.*"

THERE WAS a wide-eyed wildness under her polite veneer. He wouldn't have minded being the one who tamed her and broke her in. All four women at Savall, Ltd. were stunning—a superb combination with their lack of moral sensibility that was guaranteed by their records, ex-cons the lot of them. Their business was growing by leaps and bounds.

Samantha had something special about her that made her stand out from the others, however, and it wouldn't let him rest, had grabbed him from the beginning. She had such an abundance of nervous energy humming through her. She was forever in motion.

Cavanaugh sat behind his desk and pictured harnessing Samantha Hanley's energies for his own purposes. He didn't care about the guy she'd been with. If anything, he added to the challenge. Rivals didn't scare him, inside or outside of business.

Moretti was her lover at the moment, he was pretty sure. He'd picked up on some odd vibes between the two. They had that look of the guilty, especially Samantha, of people caught at something they shouldn't have been doing.

He was an attorney. A crooked one if he was

close to the women. Cavanaugh would bet a kilo of the best cheese he had flown in from Paris that morning that Moretti was in on the money laundering.

Everyone could always use another shady lawyer. Moretti could come in handy yet. He didn't need to know if Samantha made a few detours to the party host's bed.

And she would, Cavanaugh was pretty sure of that. Women always gravitated to the most powerful man in any group. It was part of their genetic conditioning, part of the primal program that ran in their DNA. A splendid bit of biology he regularly took advantage of.

"Last van just left," Roberto said as he came through the door. Without knocking.

Cavanaugh shrugged off the moment of annoyance. The man was all brawn but little social sensibility. Any attempt to teach him the finer points of polite behavior and manners were a waste of energy. "Good. Make sure the place is cleaned up. We have visitors coming."

"Sure, boss."

"Anything else?"

"That's it."

"I'm ready for my lunch to be sent up," he said and the man disappeared the next second— miracle of miracles, closing the door behind him.

He signed into one of his many bank accounts he kept under assumed names and filled out the online form to wire money to one of the many front businesses that, in a convoluted way, belonged to Tsernyakov. That one could be dangerous if he didn't get his full cut of the business and on time. People in his organization who didn't perform to expectations tended to disappear.

A few clicks on the keyboard concluded that business.

Cavanaugh leaned back in his chair, his lips pressed together. Having to give away his money always left a bad taste in his mouth. He shrugged it off and went back to thinking about Samantha Hanley in his bed, a much more pleasant topic.

SAM STOOD by her dresser and listened to the noises in the living room. Reese Moretti was making up the couch for himself. She'd never had a man in her apartment before. Up until a few weeks ago, she'd never had an apartment.

She took a deep breath and walked out with the pillow and blanket she was holding. Better do it before she lost her nerve.

"Here." She held out the bedding and gestured toward the couch. "Sorry, it's the best I can do."

All the women on the team got one-bedroom apartments. It hadn't seemed necessary to spring for more. They spent most of their time at the office or snooping around at the various business functions the island's elite hosted, trying to figure out who else might be doing business with Tsernyakov. The man had money coming to the island through a maze of channels. They couldn't just sit back now that they had Cavanaugh. With a guy like Tsernyakov, one needed many backup plans.

"The powder room is all yours," she said, not mentioning the obvious, that to shower he would need to use her bathroom. She'd spent an hour that morning cleaning it.

She hadn't grown up in an orderly environment and at times had trouble remembering to put things away. She was improving, though. And she had paid special attention for Reese Moretti's sake.

The idea was for the two of them to spend as much time together as possible, since, in twenty-four hours, they would have to sell Cavanaugh on the idea that they were romantically linked. That made her more nervous than the rest of the mission put together. They needed to get to know each other and become comfortable with the situation in a hurry.

"Thanks." He glanced up, looking just like David, and yet different in so many ways. He tested the couch, wearing the same grim expression as he had since his arrival a couple of hours ago—one of the many differences between the twins. David didn't do grim.

The azure-blue Naugahyde monster that came with the apartment was hard as a chunk of sidewalk. "Sorry," she said again.

"Don't sweat it. I just spent a month sleeping in the bush in Africa."

She couldn't picture David, always dressed in some sleek silk suit, say anything like that. "Under a bush?" She'd spent plenty of nights on the street; she could sympathize.

But he shook his head with a semiamused look. "*In* the bush. It's an expression. Just means out in the wild, wherever you find a convenient piece of ground when night falls."

Reese dropped the bedding at the end of the couch. His movements weren't as elegant as David's. He was more soldierlike, watchful and alert, his dark gray eyes penetrating. There was effortless strength to everything he did, his posture, his gaze; it even came through in his voice. He was clearly used to giving orders, had grilled her for a good hour after the briefing he had received from Nick Tarasov and Brant Law.

After spending most of the evening with him, skirting him warily in the small apartment, she hadn't gotten a handle on him yet.

He sat and kicked off his safari boots, then leaned back on the couch, rubbed a hand over his face as he looked around once again, his mouth set in a tight line of disapproval.

David Moretti's smooth and easygoing ways made her frazzled, but it took Reese's brusque manner to get her really nervous. David had that benign, gentlemanly air about him. Reese didn't.

"You can have the bedroom if you want." The words came out of her mouth without thought or intention.

"Sofa's fine."

"Is something wrong?" Now, why would she ask that? She should have just walked away. Her nerves made her mouth run.

He watched her carefully for a long moment before he responded. "I spent the last four months in Uganda between two rebel factions, risking my team for a man who turned out to have been dead the whole time. We came back with seven gunshot injuries between the four of us."

Clearly, he didn't want to be here. She wondered how Brant and Nick had managed to talk him into it. From the look on his face, he wasn't going to be a lot of fun to be around.

A single week, that was all. She could handle that standing on one foot. She'd been forced to put up with worse company in the past. The years she had spent at Brighton Federal Correctional Institute came to mind.

"Okay, I'll leave you to get some rest." She backed toward her bedroom.

"We don't have much time. We'd better get to work," he said, and when she looked at him blankly, added, "We are supposed to get to know each other."

What did he call the hour-long interrogation he'd put her through earlier in the kitchen? Or was he going to finally reveal more about himself? She drew a deep breath and walked back, sat gingerly in the armchair opposite him.

"Nick Tarasov tells me you're good with a gun," he said with some undisguised doubt in his voice. "He seemed confident that you could handle yourself in a hand-to-hand tussle, too, in your own weight group." He looked her over as if he was measuring her ounce by ounce and ended up with an expression that said she wasn't quite up to snuff.

She resisted the urge to pull herself taller. "I went through the training" was all she said.

He raised a dark eyebrow. "So you think you can handle whatever comes your way?"

"I'm not stupid."

The eyebrow went back down. There might have been a shadow of approval that crossed his face before he put forward his next question. "How long have we supposedly known each other?"

"Three months." That was how long she'd been out. Where had the time gone?

"How much nudity are you comfortable with?" His gaze was sharp on her face, unflinching.

The question brought her up short. What did that have to do with anything? And yet, after a second, she had to admit that the question *was* relevant. Cavanaugh thought Reese—pretending to be David—was her lover. She swallowed, her already frazzled nerves buzzing as if she were undergoing electroshock therapy. "Very little."

When you spent your teenage years on the streets, you strove to cover as much as possible, look as unappealing as possible, as scary as possible. It had been part of her defense mechanism. She'd hidden behind the darkest of Goth looks, complete with chains and studded chokers, and complemented it all with a tongue and gaze as sharp as razors.

Prison had taken away most of her props. Anita had been working on her to make her see the lack of necessity for the rest. She wasn't quite there yet, but even Sam had to admit that she *had* mellowed. She was no longer frightened of everything, so in turn she no longer wanted to frighten anyone who so much as looked at her.

The concept of nudity, however, especially in

the same context with Reese, scared her. She searched for a cutting remark to disguise that fact.

"We are going to a beach party," he said dryly before she could come up with one.

She had an image of topless cover models frolicking in the surf. Knowing Cavanaugh, it wasn't impossible.

"How far are you willing to go for this mission of yours?" Reese laid down the challenge.

Putting it that way got her back up. "I'll do what I have to."

"Good." He nodded and extended his arm toward her. "Then come and sit on my lap."

It was the wrong thing to say. She was on her feet the next second. "Touch me and lose the hand." The warning tore from her throat, hoarse and hard as a fist.

He tilted his head and waited a beat. "For the next three days, we are supposed to pretend that we are madly in lust. How do you think we'll pull that off when you look like you're ready to jump out of your skin even with three feet between us?"

She drew some air and let a couple of seconds tick by, straightened her back. Okay, so she'd overreacted. He wasn't about to jump her. And he was right, once they got to Cavanaugh's mansion, it would look suspicious if they never touched.

She had to make herself get over it.

She fisted then relaxed her hands, trying to swallow the memories in vain. She knew her face was getting whiter with every inch she moved toward him. Her muscles tensed. She stopped in front of him and fought to shrug off the temporary paralysis that clutched her.

Stop it.

This was stupid. He was Reese Moretti, the man who was going to keep her safe. He wasn't Buck. He wasn't like Buck at all.

Pretend, she told herself. *Pretend it doesn't freak you out so bad that you can barely breathe.*

She looked into his face and could no longer find the disdain he'd shown since his arrival. He was watching her with a darkening expression.

"Who was it?" he asked quietly, through clenched teeth.

She could have pretended not to understand what he was asking, but she didn't have the energy. All the starch had gone out of her, leaving her feeling weak.

"My stepfather," she said, and couldn't stop the images in her head.

Buck Cossner drank. When her mother wasn't home, he drank a lot. And when he was drunk, he got mad. When he got mad, he hit her. Then he would feel bad and want to console her, no matter how hard she tried to tell him she was okay, no matter that she never cried. She'd been more afraid of his consoling than the beating. It'd always started with, *I'm sorry, honey. Come sit on my lap.*

Chapter Two

Reese stood, and she cringed, even though there was nothing threatening in his movements. If anything, he seemed an island of calm and strength. Even the bad-tempered look that she'd thought permanent was replaced by a softer expression.

"Take it easy."

A part of her was staring at the transformation, at how handsome he was without the drawn-together brows and his mouth set in a flat, displeased line, how even the gray of his eyes changed. But the rest of her couldn't help backing away a step. In a moment of conflicting emotions, instinct honed by years of bad experiences trumped everything. Goose bumps she couldn't control rose on the bare skin of her arms.

A muscle jumped in his cheek. "Is that why you ran away from home?" Then, when she didn't respond, he said, "I read your file."

She nodded and they stood there like that, a foot or so between them. He wouldn't take his eyes off her.

And God, that felt good. Because when you lived on the streets and became one of the "undesirables" of society, the first thing everyone did was avert their eyes. Nobody wanted to see the filth or desperation, nobody wanted to risk a pang of guilt, that they should feel uncomfortable. She had spent years without ever being acknowledged by anyone except those who sought to use or abuse her. She'd been a "problem," and all people wanted was for problems to go away.

But there was no pity in Reese Moretti's gaze, nor anything remotely judgmental.

She took a breath, feeling her lungs open up. "What are we supposed to do?"

His shoulders were relaxed, as well as his commando stance. The earlier bluster seemed to disappear from his body language, but some indelible hardness remained. He considered her for a moment. "Nothing if you're not comfortable with this. We'll find a way around it."

And maybe arouse Cavanaugh's suspicion and mess up the whole operation. No way she was going to be the reason this mission failed.

The very fact that Reese gave her a way out made it possible for her to consider letting him closer.

"I'm going to have to get used to human contact." It was the healthy thing to do. She needed to get over the past in order to move into a better future. Anita had told her that during one of the woman's numerous pep talks, and Sam could see now that Anita had been right.

She took a deep breath. "Maybe we could start with…" She hesitated, and he waited. "Maybe you could just put your hands on me."

He raised a hand to her arm, keeping his gaze on her face the whole time. "I can't promise not to do anything you don't like in the next few days, but I promise I'm not ever going to do anything that would hurt you."

She nodded, nervous enough from his touch to jump all the way to the moon.

His other hand reached up to her other arm, and he rubbed the goose bumps away with his thumb. "Everything is different now. Back then, you did what you had to. You got yourself out of a bad situation. You survived. You are a hundred percent stronger now." He gave her an encouraging smile.

An actual smile. On Reese Moretti.

She was so startled, she almost believed him. She had always thought herself weak for running away instead of staying and fighting. Weak and stupid. Smart people didn't end up on the street.

A survivor. After knowing the worst of the filth about her, how could he see her like that? How could he still touch her?

She expected the cursory squeeze of polite support, then for him to let go. Instead, he drew her closer, his demeanor nonthreatening, nonsexual. And yet she felt stiff, couldn't relax, not even in response to the comfort he was offering.

Then, through the acute sense of discomfort, another feeling seeped through slowly. Surprise. His solid strength seemed like a bulwark against the world rather than suffocating restraints as it had with other men. If only she could accept it.

It's crazy. Her defenses rose. She knew next to nothing about the man.

But that inner voice that had shouted "run, run, run" for the last decade, now stayed curiously silent. After a second or two, she leaned against his shoulder and let him tighten his arms around her. Not because she was beginning to feel comfortable, but because she knew that was what a normal person would do. As long as she was aware of the normal responses and could fake them, they would be okay.

"How are you doing?" His voice was surprisingly gentle.

"Fine," she lied.

Truth was, she was unable to accept physical comfort from another person.

Anita had tried, Anita Caballo, with her over-developed sense for mothering and saving all who were around her. But Sam had always resisted even the simplest hug. She didn't trust women any more than men. Her own mother had taken off and left her with Buck at the end.

"I'm here to help you," Reese said.

"I know." She drew a deep breath and suddenly felt her eyes burning. What was wrong with her?

"You're nervous about tomorrow?" He pulled back a little. "What if I kissed your forehead?" But he didn't move.

A second or two passed before she realized he was waiting for permission.

"Okay."

His eyes were full of encouragement as he leaned over and pressed his lips above her eyebrow. He stayed there for a second before pulling away.

"See? It's not that difficult. You just have to trust me."

He was asking the impossible.

"I'll try," she said anyway. "Don't take it personally. It's—"

"Don't worry about it. I know," he said.

And from the look on his face she got a feeling that he really did. "How?"

"My job is to bring people back. Go up against

rebels, bandits, whomever. I've done a few pseudo religious sects and gangs, too, over the years. I've seen both men and women who'd gone through hell before we got to them."

They stood in silence for a while as she tried to picture the kind of work he did, the danger of it. The idea that he would do that for strangers was stunning. When she'd lived on the streets, every day she prayed for safety. She'd done dangerous things, but only out of necessity. At the end, prison had been a relief.

And look where she'd ended up now.

What if joining this mission was the worst decision she'd made yet? What if she messed up and let them all down? What if all she ended up proving, to herself and the others, was that she was a lost cause?

"How about if we just watch some TV?" he asked after a while. "You can sit by me and we'll hold hands. You can put your head on my shoulder when you get comfortable."

She nodded and sat.

He plopped down next to her and took her hand. "We can't have you jump and look ready to run every time we brush up against each other."

"I know. I can do this." She didn't want him to think she was a total incompetent idiot who was unsuitable for the mission.

"I know you can. Just relax."

It helped that he was doing just that, leaning back and surfing through the channels as if he were in his own living room—wherever he lived when he wasn't sleeping in the bush.

He settled on the National Geographic Channel. "Okay with you?"

"Sure." She watched an interview with a woman who took in orphaned lion cubs.

They were cute feeding from a bottle. She let her tightly wound muscles loosen up a little. The cubs grew and needed to be taught to hunt. That took a while. Life was a learning experience for everyone, everywhere. Sam made herself lean against the man next to her, conscious of their bodies touching, not the least comfortable, but making herself do it all the same. If she could learn to pretend, she would be happy with that.

She didn't think she could ever forget enough to have the real thing, to be able to relax around a man.

TSERNYAKOV GLANCED at his timetable and ticked off another task done. Next was calling in all debts people owed him. If they didn't pay now, they sure as hell wouldn't be able to pay next month this time. The clock was ticking.

He needed all that he could get his hands on, and not just the many currencies he did business in. After the terrorist attack, as economies collapsed, inflation was likely to soar. Whoever couldn't pay up, he would persuade to substitute hard cash with land, equipment, gold, anything potentially valuable.

He looked at his mile-long to do list, resenting that he had to handle all the work when he employed thousands. But this was information he couldn't trust to anyone.

COME ON, SAM. *Where are you?* Reese glanced toward the main house while keeping a smile on his face and his full attention, seemingly, on the blonde in front of him. The beach party was a lot smaller than they had expected. They'd figured over a hundred people. There were only about thirty, scattered in small groups on the sand.

"So what more could I do to avoid taxes?" Eva Hern didn't bat her eyes, but made long, sweeping moves with her eyelashes, many of which were the glue-on kind.

Who wore fake eyelashes to the beach? And for heaven's sake, why? He tried not to look at the little clumps of adhesive on her eyelids. Maybe he was out of step with fashion. He had no time to socialize.

"You could give all your money to charity," he said smoothly.

They both laughed. Then he did his best to give

an answer like his brother, David, the attorney whom he was impersonating, would. "I can't really tell you anything without looking at your particular situation. I'd be happy to get together with you sometime next week in your office to chat about this."

Judging from the woman's widening smile, he'd given the right answer.

"I'll call you. Definitely," she said and wiggled her shoulders. She swam topless like most of the female guests, but had put on a see-through beach shirt when she'd decided to come over and chat him up.

He made a point not to look below her eyes. It seemed to disappoint and frustrate her enough to keep her constantly moving, from pose to pose.

He glanced at his watch. Sam had been gone for twenty minutes.

Too long.

She was supposed to get in and out as fast as she could. The plan was for her to take pictures of the Cavanaugh mansion's back entry and kitchen with the micro camera she wore disguised as a large ring. She was pretending to be searching for a bottle of mineral water as they were out of "gentle" at the grass-hut bar outside.

Another thing he had missed somehow, that mineral water now came in three varieties: still (pink cap), carbonated (blue cap) and gently carbonated (green cap)—some weird stuff Cavanaugh had apparently brought in from Europe. He thought of all those times when he and his men had drunk from puddles in the jungle or sucked moisture out of roots in the desert. Different worlds for sure.

"How long are you staying on the island?" Eva was asking.

"Maybe another week," he said. He certainly had enough work to get back to.

Except for Sam, who'd turned out to be okay, he couldn't wait to be rid of this job. Going into an operation without a gun left him unsettled. They were armed only with a cell phone and a "secret weapon" that had come from one of the men on his team, Tony Ferrarella, who, in between missions, spent a lot of time in his lab, exercising his inventor genius. The can was a prototype, only with Reese by chance when he'd gotten the call from his brother and hopped the first plane to the island. He wished they had used it today. He couldn't stand not knowing what was going on in there.

The small can of what looked like breath-freshener spray contained microtransmitters too small to be seen by the naked eye. Each were too weak to work alone, but sprayed on a smooth surface they worked together to transmit voice over a hundred feet or so. They were undetectable, but highly vulnerable, good for about twenty-four hours, after which the fine sheen of dust that would naturally accumulate silenced them forever.

He caught movement from the corner of his eye at the mansion. Cavanaugh was walking out with Sam.

Reese was poised to come to her aid if she needed him, but then Sam laughed and linked her arm with Cavanaugh's.

Didn't they just look like the best of friends? What in hell had she been doing in there all this time? He reached to his chest and pretended consternation at the fact that his cell phone wasn't hanging there. He glanced toward the beach and the towel he'd been occupying, then flashed an apologetic smile to Eva.

"I'm sorry. I seem to have left my cell in the room. I'd better go up there and get it. I'm expecting a call from a client."

"You couldn't stop working just for a day or two?" Her eyes promised all kinds of incentives, although she was here at the party with her boyfriend, Derrick something or other.

"Occupational hazard," he said. "See you around?"

"You bet." She looked only slightly put out as she headed toward the beach.

She had checked out legit. He'd called in the names of the guests to Brant as soon as he'd had them.

Reese set his course toward one of the two guest bungalows that stood on either side of the Cavanaugh estate. Sam and he had been housed in the upstairs suite of the smaller. He'd seen plenty of fancy before: most of his clients had been big-time businessmen, and he'd spent time in their homes. Sam seemed uncomfortable, however, by the effortless splendor.

Not that she needed anything more to make her feel self-conscious. The woman was a bundle of nerves as it was. He wished he could think up something that would set her at ease and give her some sense of security even if just for half an hour. Then again, the middle of a dangerous recon mission was probably not the right time to relax. He really hoped she was going to be able to work out her issues and move beyond her past. When he looked at her, beyond the beauty, he saw plenty of courage and potential.

He wished he hadn't let his distaste for the FBI's strong-arm tactics show at the beginning, behaving like the morose bastard he could be when something rubbed him wrong. But he had a new client halfway across the world he was supposed to save. And would the FBI just give him the information he needed to do his job? Hell, no. They dangled it in front of him, forcing him to take on this mission first, stuff that had nothing to do with him. He'd been annoyed and let it show, and had probably scared her, which had been the flat-out stupidest thing to do considering her past and the fact that they were supposed to be a team.

He slipped inside the house and went up the stairs, waited for her in the living room. *Be nice.*

But then he laid eyes on her slim figure as she came in and it hit him what Cavanaugh could have done to her, alone in the big house. How the hell was he supposed to protect her when his hands were tied by the instructions he'd been given— *protect without interfering.* What kind of insane guideline was that?

"What took you so long?" He could have kicked himself at how harsh his voice sounded.

She cast him a wary glance. "I ran into Philippe."

He had checked their room for listening devices the first day they'd gotten there and rechecked again every single day. So far it seemed their host wasn't snooping on his guests, so they could speak freely.

"I saw." He hadn't missed the prolonged looks earlier either and the always too-bright smiles, Cavanaugh's frequent excuses at conversation. He couldn't blame the man, but he wasn't going to let whatever the guy thought would happen go anywhere. Sam didn't need that kind of harassment.

He hadn't been too fond of the mission at the beginning, but he was really starting to hate it now that he'd met Cavanaugh and his goons. Any way he looked at it, the women were being used in a dangerous game.

Sam skirted by him toward the kitchen, and his gaze fell to her lower back, to the tattoo of a rose closed tight in a bud, the short stem having some pretty nasty-looking thorns. She stopped and drew a breath, turned to look him in the eye. He recognized the moment for what it was, her decision not to let him intimidate her. She had plenty of sheer guts, this one. He put the frown away.

"So I saw Eva keeping you company," she remarked with a smirk before continuing to the kitchen to search the fridge. She ate on the hour, every hour. Not that any of it stuck to her.

"She wanted free tax advice," he said, meaning to move away, but his attention stayed fixed on Sam.

She wore a tasteful bikini that covered everything and still managed to entice more than all the bare flesh on the sand. She had hair a startling color of Irish red, falling in soft waves to just below her ear, as well as big, luminous green eyes shining out of her face. She had no shortage of guys coming over to meet her on the beach.

She played along, even flirting on occasion, although he was pretty sure that was all bravado and she couldn't have followed through if her life depended on it. She was uncomfortable around men with hunger in their eyes, but was good at hiding that fact and never let her unease stop her from doing her job.

He made a point of sticking by her as much as he could. He would have thought the two of them coming together, rooming together, sent a message to the others, but it seemed the standard rules of society were not strictly kept on private beaches.

"So what have you got?" he asked, returning to the business at hand. He tossed himself into the armchair by the window, slumped deep, arms and legs open, his body language as easygoing as he could make it.

She seemed to relax in response, leaning against the counter. "He showed me around downstairs." She grinned, looking pretty pleased with herself.

"Pictures?"

"I got everything." She licked some thick sugary cream off her bottom lip. "You sure you don't want one?" She extended the plate of goodies toward him.

He shook his head.

"Okay, almost everything." She stuck the plate

back into the fridge. "There were a couple of closed doors he didn't elaborate on."

"We'll start our search there. You should put on more sunscreen." Her shoulder was getting a pink tinge to it. She was fair skinned. He looked away.

"I should try to get back in. I could pretend to need extra towels."

"The guesthouse has its own linen closet."

"I'll say I couldn't find it."

They'd been shown around a couple of hours ago, upon their arrival, but the place really was big enough to forget some of it. Still, if she kept coming up to the mansion, someone might think it suspicious.

"We do it together. Tonight," he said.

THE DRINKING PICKED up as the sun went down. Cavanaugh had brought in a local band to play Caribbean tunes mixed with popular French music. He spent a fair amount of time with his guests, but disappeared inside his house now and then.

Was he conducting business? Did he have something big going down? Was it connected to Tsernyakov?

Sam glanced across the sand and her gaze met Reese's. He nodded slowly. It was near midnight. Time for them to get started.

She walked up to him and stepped behind him

as he chatted with a small group, put her arms around his waist and leaned against his back. She was comfortable with this much.

He covered her hands with his own. "Hi."

She tugged on reflex, expecting to feel trapped, then caught herself and went still. "Want to go for a walk on the beach?"

He turned and smiled at her. "Sure." He extricated himself from the conversation and grabbed on to her hand as he led her toward where the waves met the white sand glowing in the moonlight.

"Have you seen Cavanaugh?" she asked. She'd been wandering around the property, trying to spot him for the last hour.

"He went out on the speedboat with a couple of women a while ago."

So that had been him. She'd been too far away at the time to see.

The breeze was gentle and still warm, the sand soft under her bare feet. Now and then she had to jump to get out of the way of an overreaching wave. The flower print, wrap-style skirt hung to her ankles, stroking her skin with each step.

That she would feel comfortable in clothes like these surprised her, having dressed for years in nothing but black, accessorizing with chains, spiking her hair, building an armor around her from clothes and attitude. She didn't miss the whole Goth look. Odd that she couldn't remember when she'd begun feeling comfortable without it.

The breeze blew the material of her skirt against Reese's legs from time to time. She adjusted her hand in his. Now that she was more comfortable around him, she didn't mind the physical contact as much. She could see why some women thought it nice.

A sense of contentedness filled her without warning. Then, self-consciousness. Was this how normal people felt when they were out on a moonlit night? The thought brought a sudden, breathtaking need for life, her life, to be as normal as that. Could she ever achieve it? What would it take to make it happen?

"Let's start walking up." Reese led her toward the line of palm trees that separated Cavanaugh's property from his neighbor's ostentatious palace.

The trees widened into a little grove with a few hammocks strung between the trunks. If anyone was watching them, a man and a woman heading that way would look anything but suspicious.

Another couple had thought of utilizing the area already, it seemed. One of the hammocks was occupied and swaying suggestively. They passed in a wide arc around it.

A stone path began at the other end of the grove, leading to the pool. They took it.

"Should we spend a few minutes here?" she asked, nervous all of a sudden.

He put his arms around her and turned her in a circle, pretending to pay attention only to her, while effectively surveying their surroundings. "I don't think that's necessary. Nobody seems to be watching."

They rounded the pool and reached the terrace attached to the main house. It was circled with stone columns and potted palms and was set up for dining, with elegantly carved teak chairs and tables.

"Let's settle down here for a second." Reese pulled a chair out for her. "See any of Cavanaugh's men?"

She scanned the area. "No."

"Good. Me, neither." He nodded toward the French doors upstairs, which opened onto the balcony. Sheer white curtains moved in and out in the breeze. "Point of entry?"

She glanced to the downstairs entrance and the camera above it. There was nothing above the upstairs door. They probably figured anyone trying to get up there would be recorded by the downstairs system anyway.

Reese reached over the table and took her hand, rubbed his thumb over it before he stood. She got to her feet and let him pull her against him.

"So, what's the plan?" she asked into his neck.

"We're going to make out behind that column." He turned her a little then was moving that way already.

Even knowing he didn't really mean it, her blood sped to a rush. She swallowed and tried to act nonchalant, knowing that she could fool the cameras, but she wasn't fooling him.

He began by rubbing his lips along the side of her cheek. She stopped in her tracks from the shock of sensation and realized that was just what he wanted. He nudged her against the column gently, keeping his gaze on hers, making sure he wasn't pushing her panic button. And she couldn't be scared knowing just how much energy he spent on making sure she was comfortable.

He looked up then stood still for a second, seeming to be plotting something.

"The column and this potted palm are keeping us from view of the camera," she said.

"Right. You're going to climb me to get up to the balcony."

She closed her eyes for a moment. She didn't mind the breaking-and-entering part. Climbing Reese Moretti was another matter. A couple of seconds passed before she could say, "Okay."

"Be careful," he said and put his hands on her waist, then he was lifting her.

The wraparound skirt opened conveniently,

giving her plenty of room to maneuver with her legs, using her feet for support on Reese's shoulders. Then her hands closed around the railing and she pulled. He pushed his palms under her soles and helped her up.

"Okay," she whispered and crept to the French doors for a look before returning to him. "Nobody's here."

He stood by the column, his hands braced on each side. His shoulders were wide enough so the camera would see those. As long as he stayed that way, anyone watching on the security monitor would think he had her in front of him, pinned.

"I'll be right back." She crossed the balcony again and went in low, finding herself in what looked to be a spare bedroom for the mansion.

She gave it a quick check and took a few pictures with her camera ring before moving on. She poked her head out the door. If someone saw her, she could pretend she had snuck into the mansion to seek out Cavanaugh. With Cavanaugh's interest in a wide variety of women, her presence wouldn't require any further explanation for his staff.

But the hallway was empty. She stepped outside.

There were motion sensors in the corner of the ceiling, but they had figured the system wouldn't be turned on until the fun for the day ended and the guests were settled into their bungalows for the night. Since the room she'd breached was at the end of the hallway, she had only one way to go: forward. Two doors stood on her right, one on her left. She cracked each as she passed by. One was a home gym, one a bathroom, another a cleaning closet.

The hallway came out to an open area with cathedral ceilings and a view to a sprawling living room below that she remembered from her earlier visit. She stayed near the wall so she wouldn't be seen if someone walked in downstairs.

She put her hand on the next door and tried to push it open. She couldn't. *This is it.* The place wouldn't be locked if Cavanaugh wasn't hiding something here. She pulled out the micro tool kit that had been hidden in the ostentatious, shell-covered barrette in her hair.

The door had two locks, one built into the doorknob and one at about eye level. Trickier than what she had been used to when she had lived on the streets and had, at times, been forced to break the law for food. Or while in foster care, when she'd had to break out of the various rooms, basements, attics and toolsheds she'd been locked inside. The fancy tool kit felt foreign, too, although she had been practicing.

She was fairly certain she'd gotten the top lock

open, but she wasn't getting anywhere with the one on the bottom. Something was clicking. She had to be on the right track. Then it hit her. Both pegs had to be turned at the same time.

And then she was in, careful to open the door only a few inches should there be motion sensors inside. She put her eye to the crack.

The room was windowless, pitch-dark other than the light filtering through the small opening of the door. She could make out a desk with a computer, filing cabinets against the walls, a couple of fax machines and a giant shredder. A red laser light cut through the darkness less than an inch from the door's edge.

She could see only half the room like this, but to open the door enough to stick her head inside would set off the alarm. It was a miracle she hadn't set if off already.

She took a small step back just as the sound of feet drumming on stairs hit her ears.

Chapter Three

Even with her heart doing backflips in her throat, she had enough presence of mind to lock the door behind her exactly as she had found it. Then she took off down the hallway. She didn't make it to the end room.

As Sam turned back, she could see the tops of the heads of the men who were coming up. The cleaning closet seemed her only option. She practically hurled herself inside.

The space was dark and tight, smelling like bleach and citrus-scented cleaning solution. She stayed still, not daring to make any noise. The door didn't block much. She could hear everything the two men were saying.

"Saw the blonde? Man, she's stacked. Wouldn't mind if she tripped and fell on top of me."

"What's stopping you from tripping and falling on top of her?" The other one laughed.

"Her husband is here."

"I bet Philippe had her already."

"So what?" The first guy sounded annoyed. "He's the boss. He always gets what he wants."

Dissent in the ranks? She stored the information for later. They never knew what could come in handy down the road.

A door opened and closed, then she could no longer hear the men. How long should she wait? Would they stay wherever they'd gone, or would they be coming back in a few seconds? She was prepared to act like an Oscar winner if she was caught, but it would have been much better for her and the mission if she made her way out of the mansion unseen.

Sam emerged from her hiding place with caution. The hallway was empty. She made her way to the back bedroom as fast as she could.

She pushed the door open and whispered, "Philippe," to play out her role of hussy-in-search-of-illicit-pleasure, but nobody was in there. Looked like the men had gone to the gym. She let out the breath she'd been holding, then she was through the room and out on the balcony, lowering herself into Reese's waiting arms.

"Everything okay?" He didn't look pleased at having had to stay behind.

"Found his office. I'll have to get back in there again."

"He's right. Enough is enough." A stranger's voice came from around the corner. The next second, one of Philippe's men, Roberto, rounded the building, talking on his cell.

She pressed against Reese and lifted her mouth to his, keeping her eyes open only enough to see the guy slow in her peripheral vision.

Reese didn't miss a beat. He let his lips linger. She was getting familiar with the feel of them, not exactly at ease but not scared stiff, either. He got hold of her hand and moved forward, pulling her behind him. They went only as far as the nearest hammock, where he fell back into the comfort of the ropes and pulled her on top of him.

Oh.

She held on as they swayed, feeling awkward, the urge to flee coming on.

He must have felt her body stiffen because he went completely still. "So this stepfather of yours, he's still alive?" he whispered, his voice low and tight.

What did it matter? "No." Her lawyer had told her that. Since she'd been underage at the time of her arrest, the court had attempted to reach her mother and the man she was still married to on paper. Her stepfather was gone. Her mother couldn't bother to come to her arraignment or her trial, even though a parent who pledged to resume supervision could have eased her sentence.

A few silent moments passed, then he ran a calming hand down the back of her arm, adjusting his body to balance them, to make her more comfortable. "Is Cavanaugh's goon still here?" The way they were positioned, he couldn't see for himself.

She looked from the corner of her eye. "Standing and staring."

"Might as well relax. We could be here for a while."

He linked his arms behind her waist. Oddly, it didn't make her freeze in terror. She was getting used to him, to his touch, to his scent, beginning to accept the idea he meant no harm. That she was able to relax around him, something she hadn't been able to say about another man for nearly a decade, took her by surprise each and every time.

He was different from any guy she had ever known. She didn't want to think about that, wasn't ready to consider the implications.

"I didn't get far," she whispered, needing to return her thoughts to the job. She'd mapped a single hallway—didn't even get to search the office, nor go downstairs to those doors Cavanaugh hadn't shown her earlier.

"Yeah, but you hit pay dirt. I'm guessing we'll find some interesting things in Philippe's desk when we get the chance. We know where it is now. We know what's in the room, the layout."

"I saw two guys who were up there to use Cavanaugh's private gym. Can't remember seeing them before, but we probably haven't seen all his goons yet. They seem to be working in shifts."

"Glad they didn't see you." His hot breath tickled her ear, so she shifted position, setting the hammock swinging again. Shoes crunched gravel underfoot. Roberto was moving on.

He seemed to be an important member of Cavanaugh's security team. He was always visible, always watching, making his rounds. He seemed to take himself as seriously as if he were part of the Secret Service.

Sam lifted her head and looked around. "Should I try to get back in now?"

"Not tonight." Reese sat with her. "It might look too suspicious if we got caught loitering this close to the house twice in the same night. We have the whole week to get what we want. Let's not blow anything the first day."

She slipped out of the hammock and he came after her, looped his arms around her waist. She made herself relax against him and held the pose, allowing him time to check for any danger.

None of Cavanaugh's men were in sight.

"Let's go down to the beach," he said as he broke away and took her hand. "We'll see what we can find out about Philippe from his friends."

REESE LEANED against the windowsill of the bedroom he shared with Sam, squinting against the sun, thinking about what Sam had seen at the mansion the day before. All good information, but not enough. He hated operating without knowing the parameters.

Who the hell was this guy Philippe? Some bigtime businessman the FBI was working on bringing down for some reason or other—that was all Reese had been told by his brother and two other men he'd met over the phone and never seen face-to-face.

His mission with Sam was the information-gathering sort. He was familiar with reconnaissance. He was familiar with the need-to-know basis for dissemination of information. It ticked him off that whoever ran this operation didn't think he needed to know more than the threadbare report he'd been given.

He would have never sent any of his men blindly into a situation.

He watched from behind the curtains as Sam tanned herself next to Philippe on the sand. The man was on his side, supported by an elbow, feasting his eyes on her from head to toe as they chatted. Sam had her eyes closed against the sun, looking like she had that morning when Reese had watched her sleep. As part of their cover they had to share a bed, an inconvenience that both were professional enough to handle regardless of personal preference.

Philippe reached out and drew a finger along her arm. Her eyes popped open.

He expected her to slap the man's hand away, recognized the strain in her body even from this far. Instead, she smiled up at Philippe in a way that made Reese tense.

Cavanaugh said something.

She responded, keeping the smile.

What were they talking about? He gripped the windowsill and took a deep breath. He was here to give Sam backup security. He had to allow her to conduct her mission.

Philippe's finger reached her shoulder and crossed over to her collarbone, then down the middle of her chest until it hooked on to the string that held the cups of her bikini together.

A muscle twitched in Reese's face.

Then Philippe sat up and so did Sam. And when the man started out toward the main house, Sam followed.

How long could she play along? Long enough, Reese thought. She would do it even if it killed her, to get the information her team so desperately seemed to need. She was tough like that, a quality he admired in her, even if at the moment he wished she had a little less of it. He wouldn't have minded if she told Philippe she had some other pressing need just now and backed out from the guided tour of the man's bedroom.

Reese crossed the suite and jogged down the stairs, hating that all he could do was watch. He wanted to stay close to the mansion if they were going in there. In his line of work, he rescued people. He didn't stand back and let them walk into danger.

This mission was going to drive him crazy before it was over.

He went as close as he could without looking suspicious and settled into a beach chair, angling it so that he had a full view of the mansion's front door. Then he waited. Five minutes passed. Ten. He shifted in his seat. What was taking them so long? Twenty minutes ticked by. Was she in trouble? Did she need his help?

If he went in there now, looking for her, acting the jealous boyfriend, he could ruin whatever she was setting up.

He glanced at his watch then pulled his cell

phone from his pocket, glancing around to confirm that none of the staff or the other guests were anywhere within hearing distance. He was willing to give Sam five more minutes. In the meantime, he had someone in mind to vent his frustration on.

"It's me," he said as soon as his brother, David, picked up.

"Everything okay?"

"What was the logic behind this? To blackmail some woman into using her body to get information from scum like Cavanaugh?" He was careful to keep his voice down.

"She isn't being blackmailed," David said calmly.

"Right. But if she doesn't do what you want, she goes back to prison."

"And she wasn't asked to use her body," David went on.

"She's here based on her looks as much as anything else. Have you and your FBI buddies considered what this is doing to her?"

There was a moment of silence on the other end. "Look, she lived on the street for years—"

That blew his fuse. "Oh, okay. That's different then. So she's likely been exploited before. It's fine to do it again. You're right."

"Calm down. Let her do her work."

"She's twenty-two, for heaven's sake." Just

turned a week ago. That had been in her file, too. "If you think I'm going to stand back and let her be raped—because that's what it would be, with the FBI holding her down—you picked the wrong man for the job." He slammed the phone closed as he pushed away from the chair and started out for the mansion.

THE GOOD NEWS WAS, she was in Cavanaugh's bedroom, an arm's length from his laptop on the nightstand. The bad news was, she was in Cavanaugh's bedroom, an arm's length from his bed.

And from the way he was looking at her, it was clear he expected her to end up in it.

Sam walked to the window, wishing she had on something more substantial than a bikini. "What a breathtaking view," she said.

"You should see the sunrise from here." He came up close behind her.

She turned her head, giving him a flirtatious smile. "I don't think David would like it if I stayed that long." She couldn't outright reject him. She needed to stay at the mansion, at the party, as long as she could, find out as much information as she could. The team needed Cavanaugh to like her, like them all, to do business with them, to refer Tsernyakov to them eventually. He was their sole link to the man. They couldn't afford to lose him.

And right now, it was all up to her. She could not say yes to the man, could not make herself do it regardless of what was at stake. But to say no might have a disastrous effect on the mission. Her job was to perform a very believable "maybe later."

Cavanaugh put a hand on her shoulder. "What David doesn't know, doesn't hurt him, *n'est-ce pas?*"

"And your girlfriends?" She gestured toward the bathing beauties on the beach. She'd seen several in Cavanaugh's company before.

"Just friends." He shrugged. "Nobody serious."

"Too much work and not enough time for love?" she asked jokingly.

He inclined his head. "Maybe that, too. A little bit. The truth is, it has been a long time since I've met anyone who intrigued me sufficiently. Until now."

She only half listened as she surreptitiously scanned the room and caught a glimpse of a painting of a sailboat on the wall that didn't quite lay flush. Was there something behind the picture? A safe?

Philippe's hand slid to her lower back and traced her rose tattoo.

She held herself still against the impulse to escape.

"You are more than you seem at first glance," he whispered. "You have passions and secrets and fears."

Fear was on top at the moment. Fear that he might have seen too much on her face, that he sensed too much and knew she was here under false pretenses. She looked into his watery brown eyes and prepared to give the performance of her life.

"You overestimate me." She did her best to look flirtatious while she said the words.

"I don't think so." He leaned in.

"You're—" She stepped back, couldn't help it.

"I'm what?"

She forced an embarrassed laugh. "Overwhelming," she said. "I've never met anyone like you before."

He was smiling then, too, his expression switching from disappointed to pleased. "Maybe I am." He watched her. "Maybe you could get used to me."

"Good things are easy to get used to. Isn't that what they say?"

His response was preempted by sounds of an argument from below. She recognized Reese's voice.

"I think David is looking for me." She moved toward the door.

"Of course." He got there first and opened it for her. "We shouldn't keep him waiting."

Reese stood at the bottom of the stairs, locked in a staring contest with one of Philippe's men. Roberto, was it? Then he looked up, his eyes narrowing as he watched them descend the stairs.

"Is there a problem, David?" Cavanaugh asked cordially, playing the perfect host.

She smiled at Reese, wanting him to know that everything was okay, willing him not to start anything. He wasn't supposed to come after her in the first place. What was he doing here?

"Just looking for my girl," he said, and schooled his features into an expression a shade more polite than before.

"We've been talking about the views of the ocean from the house and I showed her my favorites." Cavanaugh gestured toward the upstairs rooms. "Are you enjoying yourself here?"

Roberto was giving Sam an odd look. Was he mad at her because her boyfriend barged into the house? He'd just have to get over it. She turned her back on him and moved next to Reese, linking her arm with his, sending a silent message. *Please behave.*

"The place is amazing," he said.

She held back her sigh of relief.

"I'm glad you like it." Cavanaugh nodded, dismissing them, moving on toward the back of the house where the kitchen was.

Reese tugged her gently toward the door and she followed. Their walk back to the bungalow was short and strained.

"What happened?" he asked as soon as they were inside.

"He has a laptop and possibly a wall safe in his bedroom," she said.

Instead of being pleased at the discovery, his expression turned dark. "In his bedroom? Is that where you've been?"

"I'm here to get information." She didn't need him putting her on the defensive.

"You're not here for— Dammit." He walked to the window and looked out. A couple of seconds passed before he turned back to her, his gaze boring into hers. "Did he touch you?" he asked in a deceptively calm voice.

She shrugged. "So what?"

"Did he—"

"I didn't have sex with him if that's what you want to know," she said, angry now as she walked to the closet, grabbed a long T-shirt and pulled it over her head. "And you're here to protect me, not judge me," she added, although to be fair, he had never judged her, not once since they had met.

He stepped closer to her, looking calmer now. "I was just worried. That's all."

Okay. She took a deep breath. She didn't want

to fight with him, especially since she had been relieved to see him. "So what are we going to do about the safe?"

From the look on his face, it was clear that he recognized her attempt to distract him. "I'll take a look at it."

That sounded dangerous. "I don't think you should sneak into the house. If they catch you— I mean, if they catch me—they'll just think I'm there to—"

"What, give the lord of the manor his due?" His bad temper had returned. He threw his hands into the air in a gesture of frustration, then let them drop. "The deal is off. I'm not watching you from afar and providing only backup."

"That's what you agreed to with Brant and Nick and the others." She didn't want him to change the rules now. She didn't want to mess up. "You were at the mansion with me last night, weren't you?"

"I was hugging a stupid column outside while you were risking your life in there. Next time you go anywhere dangerous, I'll be right next to you. We do this together or not at all."

"You don't even know what it's about," she shot back, her frustration matching his now.

Then again, truth be told, she probably didn't know everything, either. She had a feeling the government only told the team as much as they absolutely had to.

"Then why don't you tell me?" He was close enough now to touch.

"I'm not authorized."

He spoke the words slowly. "Do you want to live?"

She looked away from his burning gaze. He was too intense, a live wire, too powerful. She'd had an easier time handling Cavanaugh. She wondered if anyone had ever managed to handle Reese Moretti.

"They showed you my file," she said after a while.

He nodded. "I'm not dumb enough to go into a dangerous situation with someone I know nothing about."

"You know about Philippe."

"Some," he said. "I'm beginning to think this mission is a whole lot bigger deal than my brother let on when he roped me into it."

She moved away from him and walked to the window. "He didn't think you would take it on."

He was silent for a long second. "I had a favor to ask in return."

"About a client?"

"My team is looking for someone. I thought the FBI had information they weren't sharing. When David told me he was working with the Bureau on this, I figured we could make an even trade."

"Shouldn't you be on some mountaintop tracking down kidnappers?"

"My team is there. If I can get that information from the FBI, I can save everyone a lot of grief. It's well worth the week this is taking me out of the action."

She tucked her hair behind her ear, thinking it odd how this undercover op was *out of the action* for him, while for her it was more action than she'd ever wanted. She hadn't liked being in Philippe's bedroom earlier.

From the time she'd been a teenager, she'd craved "safe." She hadn't found that at home, or in foster care, or on the streets, or in prison. And there sure wasn't anything safe about her situation here. Truth be told, the safest she felt in a long time was when she was near Reese Moretti.

"Would you really leave? If I said we were doing this my way?" She turned back to him.

He was moving toward her, stopped, took a breath then let it out. "No."

She let herself relax a little.

"But we are going to do this the safest way possible and that is for us to work together. Let's scratch the backup thing, okay?"

He phrased that as a question, but she didn't fool herself by thinking she had a choice. The decision had been made. It was written all over his face. "You're stubborn." Not to mention high-handed.

"And that's a bad quality?" A ghost of a smile played about his lips. "Not anything like you, is it?"

She bit back a grin. Okay, so she had a stubborn streak, too. Point taken.

"I can handle this," she said, not sure if she was trying to convince him or herself. After all, how many things had she gotten right in life lately?

He held her gaze. "You can. But I'll be there with you all the same."

Chapter Four

In the end, the following night they ended up investigating the boathouse. Cavanaugh had some business emergency and excused himself from his guests, sequestering himself in the mansion. They couldn't very well break into his office while he was in it.

"Tell me again what we are doing here?" Reese asked.

"Looking for evidence of drug running. I'm thinking it would be best if when Tsernyakov went down, Cavanaugh went with him."

"And your team doesn't have enough on him yet?"

"White-collar crimes." She made a face. "Real-estate speculation and money laundering. His connections would cover that up too easily. He is friends with just about every important person on the island. It would take something more serious to put him away for good."

"And Anita and Brant think Cavanaugh is in the drug business?"

She nodded, keeping to the shadows as they crept toward the building. "They did seaside surveillance a couple of weeks ago and saw a ship dropping off suspicious packages."

"I still don't think this is a good idea."

Yeah, he'd made sure she knew that.

"Catching Cavanaugh at drug running is not a priority. And if we get caught out here, we could get—kicked out."

She knew he'd been about to say killed. "What if the drugs are his connection to Tsernyakov?"

"I thought Tsernyakov did weapons?"

"Tsernyakov does everything."

She stopped as one of Cavanaugh's men came out of the house, plodded across the driveway and got into a dark pickup truck parked near the entrance. The gate opened for him silently.

"I wonder where he's going," he said as he pulled his cell from his pocket.

"Who are you calling?"

"Law," he said, and Brant Law must have picked up immediately because he gave a quick description of the car and which way it turned when it left the property.

They stopped when they reached the boathouse. Sam tried the door. Locked. That didn't pose much of a problem. She got them in under thirty seconds.

The place was empty, nothing but boating equipment, shelves of varnishes, a stack of life vests, pulleys and some kind of lifting mechanism with a small motorboat suspended from it. She couldn't make out much more than that at first glance. The small windows provided little light, and they couldn't flip the switch by the door without alerting everyone to their presence.

A long table took up the end of the building, reaching from wall to wall. That was where Reese headed. She followed, noting the metal boxes under the table, each one padlocked. She took out her tool kit and popped the lock. Reese dug in.

"You were right," he said.

"What is it?" She expected a brick of heroin, and was surprised when he pulled out a fistful of empty Ziploc bags. She reached for the next box. It had a half dozen of those digital kitchen scales in it. "Redistribution center," she said.

The one thing she hadn't gotten into when she'd lived on the streets was drugs, but she'd seen enough of the business to know what was what. She held out her ring to take a picture. "Probably not enough light."

Reese pulled a sheet of aluminum that was stuck between the table and the wall and held the shiny metal up so it reflected all the light from the window to the spot where she needed it.

He was resourceful, she had to give him that. A good quality in a partner.

"Thanks." She snapped two pictures only. The tiny camera's memory wasn't endless and they still had to search Cavanaugh's office and bedroom.

"Hear that?" Reese lifted a hand to caution her to silence. He slipped the sheet of aluminum back in place.

Faint sounds came from outside. Sam glanced around for a place to hide.

"What idiot left this open?" The voice coming from the door startled her into action. She stepped up on the table then dived into the motorboat, Reese right behind her. She was lying on something hard that dug into her ribs, but didn't dare move. Reese reached up to the pulley to stop the boat from swaying. He just managed when the lights came on.

"Move it, kid," the same voice, Roberto's, said, and there was some scuffle.

"I didn't do it, man." The second voice was young and desperate.

"Don't worry about it, you'll be fine."

"Can you untie me?"

"No can do. The boss wants to make sure you stay here."

"I will, I swear, man. I'm not gonna do anythin' stupid."

Some odd sounds came from below, then, "You already did."

"Louise's a lyin' bitch. You gonna believe her over me?"

"Fact is, stuff did disappear."

"I'm tellin' you, man, I gave it to her. All of it."

"Then you have nothing to worry about," Roberto said from the door again. "The boss will hear you out. I'll be back in a couple of hours once all his guests go to bed."

With that, the light went out and the door closed.

"Don't leave me here, man!" the kid yelled below, then swore over and over again.

Sam remained motionless, fairly certain that the boss would not let the kid explain and escape in a couple of hours. Once the guests had gone to bed, Cavanaugh's men would probably take him out in a boat. He would never return.

The big bosses didn't forgive dirty runners. They didn't care to find out the truth. You got fingered, you were made to disappear. She'd met kids at various shelters who had ended up like that.

The one down below knew it, too. A few moments of silence passed before she could hear the sound of sniffling.

She lifted her upper body, slowly, despite Reese's restraining hand that tried to push her back. She came up just enough to see a boy of sixteen or so tied to a chair. He was crying.

They were trapped. All three of them.

SHE WAS GOING to do something stupid like try to save the kid, who would in turn tell Cavanaugh all about them to save his own skin, no doubt. Reese shook his head.

Even in the semidarkness, he could see the fire in her glare.

She gestured toward the kid.

He shook his head again.

The sound of scraping came from below. He looked over the edge of the boat. The boy was trying to get out from under the ropes. He gave up after about a minute. He was tied with good sail ropes and expert seaman ties. He tried to drag the chair to the door. After a yard or so, the leg got caught on something and he tripped, fell on his face. He swore and cried again, at the same time. Reese could smell his desperation from across the room.

A half hour passed before the kid made it to the

door. Then he tried to open it with his mouth. That didn't work. Turning the knob wasn't enough. It was locked from the outside. He wasn't going to pick that lock with his teeth.

Sam nudged Reese with her feet. Like he needed another reminder that he was on top of her; every curve that he'd spent considerable energy ignoring day in and day out pressed against him in an intimate way. She shifted and he ground his teeth together, reminding himself that she only wanted one thing from him. He shook his head with as much emphasis as he could muster. They held a glaring contest that lasted several minutes and included a lot of silent gesturing.

When he looked back out again, the kid was slumped forward with his head leaning against the door. He wasn't moving. His back rose and fell evenly.

Had he exhausted himself to sleep?

Even if he had, they couldn't get out without waking him. He was blocking the door.

Reese made a small noise that could have been attributed to the wind outside. The kid didn't look up. He made a louder noise. The boy remained sleeping.

Sam was sitting up now and watching, too. "We have to help him," she whispered.

Yes. In a perfect world that would have been possible. But his world was far from perfect, and he had learned long ago that he couldn't save everyone. "And put you at risk?"

"If we leave him, he'll die."

"Maybe he'll talk himself out of trouble."

Sam gave him a look full of disappointment.

For some reason it dug under his skin. What did he care what she thought of him? Why was a teenage dealer so important to her all of a sudden? Important enough to risk her life, and the lives of hundreds or thousands perhaps if this ended up blowing their cover and making the mission impossible. If they didn't get to Tsernyakov and he was allowed to continue his activities, there would be a body count that would make a single casualty pale in comparison.

But as he watched her watching the kid, he suddenly understood. It could have been her. If she'd stayed on the streets, who knew where she would have ended up?

He drew a slow breath, considered his options then gestured for her to stay before silently lowering himself to the ground. He crept to the boy, step by careful step, drew the small pocketknife from his pants and, as gently as he could, began to saw the rope.

The kid must have had an exhausting day. He remained passed out.

A little more. There. Reese sliced the last of the

rope through, pocketed the knife then stole back to the boat, hoping he hadn't just made a huge tactical mistake. But the gleam in Sam's eyes when he got back felt good. She was smiling from ear to ear.

Reese banged his hand on the side of the boat.

The chair scraped below. The boy had come awake. He could hear the door handle rattle, then footsteps across the room, noise at the table.

The kid was climbing the table to get to the window above it. But from that elevated position he would be able to see straight into the boat.

Reese looked at Sam, mouthing, "Close your eyes." Some people could sense if they were being watched. He shut his lids, too, and went limp on top of her. If the kid did look, in the darkness he might mistake them for a couple of bodies. Shouldn't find that completely out of the realm of possibility if he'd worked in the drug trade long enough.

But no gasp of surprise came from the direction of the window, just the sound of it being opened, then a thump as the kid jumped to the ground below.

Reese didn't want to wait a second longer and risk Cavanaugh's men coming back and turning the place upside down. "Let's go."

They were out of the boat and at the door in seconds. To go through the window like the kid would have risked that they'd run into him. She picked the lock—pretty handy with the tools she wore in her hair, disguised as pins and a large barrette. He peered out carefully. The beach was deserted, not a guest in sight; even the night owls had retired to their rooms, it seemed. Sam followed him as he crept from the boathouse to the nearest patch of shadows, making his way back to their bungalow.

They got about halfway and made it to the spot where they would have to come out into the open, when Sam tugged on his arm.

Cavanaugh's men were coming back.

THEY WERE TRAPPED in the bushes. Sam pressed closer to Reese, to the comfort of his bulk, and watched as the two men went into the building then a second later came running out. Both were on their cell phones, spreading out, searching the grounds. A few moments later, more men came from the house.

They ran toward the beach. Did the footprints from the window lead that way?

Sam pulled Reese through the bushes to the other side. Twenty feet of open patio lay between them and the guest bungalow. The light over the front door was on. They were sure to be seen if they went that way.

"Not there," Reese whispered as he passed her, heading toward the side that was mostly in shadow.

She followed him to a small shed, took his hand so he could help her up after him. They made it to a windowsill, hoping the air conditioner would drown out any noise they made. Then they slipped over to a balcony. Not theirs.

Roberto ran across the sand below them.

She held her breath and flashed Reese a "Now what?" look.

He gestured toward the doors.

At least they had one piece of good luck tonight. The white French doors were open. But just because the light wasn't on inside, it didn't mean nobody was awake.

In fact, the bed was decidedly squeaking.

She got down on her hands and knees. Reese rolled his eyes, but did the same. And then they went in.

If this suite was anything like theirs, the front door opened from the small foyer area right outside the bedroom. All they had to do was make it past the bed.

Moan, moan, squeak, squeak, moan, moan.

There seemed to be a lot of that going on at Cavanaugh's weeklong party. His guests were by no means inhibited.

Sam held her breath as she made her way

forward, froze when the noises stopped for a second, went weak with relief when they resumed again.

The few minutes it took to get back to their suite felt like hours. But they were finally there, the door locked between them, and she could breathe easier.

"Looked like those two were having fun," she said as she went for a glass of water to cover up her nerves, which were still far from calm. It had been a busy night.

"Those three," Reese said with amused nonchalance.

She swallowed the wrong way and coughed.

"You okay?" He was next to her in two steps.

"Fine," she said forcing out the word. "Thank you."

"Can't let my partner choke to death." A smile played above his lips.

"I meant for that boy."

"He was that important to you?" He watched her.

She nodded.

"Okay. I understand."

And the look in his eyes told her he really did. She'd never known anyone like him. Even his twin brother, and how odd was it to think this, but yes, even David with all his gleam and his suave style paled in comparison.

"So which of you was born first, you or David?" she voiced the question that came out of nowhere.

"I'm the old man." He hunched his shoulders, but grinned.

And all of a sudden, she wanted to know more about him. Anita had this game they had played when they'd first arrived on the island in hopes of forging a better team. "Tell me one thing most people don't know about you."

He straightened and looked at her thoughtfully. "In high school, I was in a garage band."

She smiled at the picture that popped into her head. "Heavy metal?"

"Country."

The smile stretched her lips wider. "With your brother?"

"With some of the neighborhood boys. David was the manager."

She shook her head. "Naturally. Sing something. Please?"

"Not even for money. I was the drummer," he said, then his eyes narrowed as he focused on her face. He reached out and brushed his thumb over her cheekbone. "You hurt yourself."

"I did?" She didn't feel a thing. She reached up, too, her fingers touching his for a split second before he pulled away. "Just dirt." She smudged her fingertips together. "Probably from when I dived into the boat."

"Crazy night, huh?"

Her gaze dropped to his lips. Like the rest of the man, they were finely cut and masculine. Then she caught herself and lifted her gaze to his and saw it darken.

And then *wa-woom*, the whole comfort thing they'd been building between them was gone. The rush of nerves and the urge to flee were back, and it confused the spit out of her. What was wrong now?

She waited for the usual icy fingers of panic that squeezed the air out of her lungs, but that didn't come. Instead, she found herself swaying toward Reese a little.

His hand slid around her waist and pulled her to him the rest of the way. When their bodies touched, it felt oddly different from before—a whole new range of sensations blinking to life throughout her body.

She was a little dizzy. And she was thirsty, definitely thirsty.

He rested his forehead against hers then shook his head as if he was fighting something. Then he gave in and touched his lips to hers.

Her eyes flew wide, then closed after a second, the lids growing unbearably heavy. Her arms were tingling right down to the tips of each finger. And then it clicked.

This is what it feels like to want a man.

The realization should have scared her, but it thrilled her instead. Because how normal was that? She was with a guy and she wanted him instead of being scared out of her brains.

And he wanted her!

The pleasure of that thought made her sink against him. She was practically swimming in relief. She smiled against his lips.

He pulled away, not looking nearly as pleased as she was. "I was going to apologize, but I see you find this funny."

"Not funny." Although she couldn't stop smiling. "Just good."

He shook his head, looking torn. "This is not what you need from me. I'm supposed to make sure you feel secure."

"You do. See? That's the point." And she was grateful for that. "I wasn't scared." Why couldn't he understand how monumental that was?

"So what did you feel?" he asked, his voice turning brusque.

"Relieved and safe." Wasn't that the most wonderful thing ever?

SHE WAS GOING to drive him crazy. Reese took in the way her face lit up, all excited because she hadn't run.

On the one hand, he understood her reaction.

Okay, almost. What the hell had just happened? When he kissed a woman he expected to make more of an impact.

Was he supposed to be overjoyed that she didn't throw up on him from nerves or run screaming into the night at the touch of his lips?

Why were *his* knees weak with wanting, dammit? Why didn't she feel the desire that was burning deep in his gut?

What right did he have to those feelings anyway?

Wrong time, wrong woman, wrong time, wrong woman. The words chimed in his head. And how many men had told themselves that right as they were whizzing down the slippery slope?

He wasn't going there. Not him. Not on this mission. He had sufficient experience to avoid that trap. He was old enough and smart enough.

"I apologize anyway." He backed up another step, wishing he could as easily back up in time. "As I said, you didn't need this now."

"But I did." She stepped right after him, full of naive enthusiasm. "I spent so much time thinking I might never be able to trust another person, that I might never have a normal reaction to a man. But you're so safe, and I'm finally starting to see that." She gave him a beaming smile.

He closed his eyes for a minute before turning around and grabbing a towel from the back of a kitchen chair.

"It didn't completely weird me out. For a moment I thought it would, but then it didn't. It just felt totally okay. You know? Like no big deal."

He could hear some frustration in her voice at his obvious lack of understanding.

He could barely understand his own reaction. When was the last time he'd felt this strong a pull toward any woman? Had he ever? Was it the adrenaline of the mission? Their forced proximity? The fact that he'd been on an overseas mission for far too long? He couldn't begin to explain. Instead, he headed for the door, grabbing his swim trunks from the back of the chair on the way.

"Reese? What are you doing?" she asked behind him, now sounding bewildered.

Did she expect him to stay and celebrate?

He *was* happy for her. It was great that he no longer scared her stiff. It was a sign of healing. She was moving in the right direction, and he wanted that for her.

But, God help him, a moment ago he had wanted so much more than that. It *would* scare her half to death to know just how much. Boy, could she learn to hate him in a hurry. He didn't have the heart to tell her that he wasn't safe, nor were his impulses where she was concerned.

So he said the only thing he could, "I'm going for a swim."

Chapter Five

Tsernyakov looked down at his list of close associates and thought long and hard about each. Which ones did he want to keep and which ones should he let be victims of the terrible attack to come? He didn't trust a single one of them; he would have been a fool to do so. But he didn't think any of them worked against him, either. If he had, he would have taken care of those already.

When this was over, would he need a bigger organization or a smaller one? Would the shake-up strengthen any of his subordinates enough so that the man might rise to become a worthy rival?

He was good at planning, but the magnitude of what was about to shake the world was, to a degree, disconcerting, even to him. He couldn't afford to miss anything. No mistakes this time. He looked at the list again. Could everyone there stand up to that kind of stress?

He picked up a pen and crossed off one name, then another. He was poised over the third when a knock on his door interrupted his thoughts.

"Come in."

"Forgive me, sir. Yakov is here."

"Send him in." He turned the paper over, leaned back in his chair and smiled.

Seeing Yakov face-to-face wasn't necessary, but he wanted to meet with the man one last time. Yakov had been a thorn in his side long enough.

"Zdrastvuitye." The man came in, pompous as ever, dressed like a billionaire. He never did know how to keep a low profile. It would have been the end of him sooner or later.

"Zdrastvuitye. How is business? Why don't you sit?" He didn't extend his hand for a shake, didn't want to overplay his role.

"Growing by the day." The man gave him a smug smile. "I heard you need me." The way he spoke the sentence made it clear how much pleasure it gave him to word it like that.

"I'm thinking about divesting a few things. You were the first man I thought of." Let his own conceit ensnare him.

He looked surprised. "Some of the shops not producing as they used to?"

Tsernyakov shrugged as if the conversation pained him. "It's getting to be too much, that's all."

"What are we talking about?"

"Not sure yet. I'll be making a list. I just wanted to know if you'd be interested in making the first bid once I'm ready to move."

"Why me?" The man's eyes narrowed.

"I do this favor and you agree not to compete against what I decide to keep." He made it sound like he was concerned about Yakov pushing him out of some markets. In reality, nobody ever came close. The areas he chose to enter, he ruled.

Yakov wasn't big enough to be called an adversary—although he liked to fancy himself as such—but he'd been the cause of considerable aggravation. Now he was hesitating, probably wary of a trap.

Tsernyakov didn't worry. Most men had one ruling emotion that outlined their actions, no matter how much they thought, how carefully they weighed. For Yakov, this was greed.

And sure enough, the man nodded after a couple of seconds. "How soon?"

"Not more than a few weeks." He watched Yakov as the man mentally calculated how much cash he could free up in that time.

I could have him killed, Tsernyakov thought idly.

He could kill the man even now, sitting across from his desk. A bullet from the handgun in his drawer would be all it took, or a nod to his secretary as he showed the man out.

But selling Yakov the assets that Tsernyakov felt were risky was so much more satisfying. He would make sure Yakov was at an impact location when The School Board unleashed their virus. The man would die a miserable death, along with his closest associates and his family, all infected by him, down to the five-legged freak cat he was rumored to have for a pet. But not before he paid a couple of million dollars to Tsernyakov for the privilege.

SAM SOAKED UP the sun as she lay on the beach and watched Cavanaugh walk toward her from the house. He hadn't shown himself all morning. Maybe he was upset over the kid's disappearance. He didn't seem upset, though, strolling down the path as if he owned the world.

A shadow fell across her face, then Reese thumped to the sand next to her.

She suppressed all thoughts of their kiss the night before. If he could pretend that nothing had happened, then so could she. She was the queen of pretending. "Go away," she said, although she wouldn't have minded his company even if all they did was lie in the sun in silence.

He looked pretty damn good in his navy blue swim shorts, even with the scars that dotted his skin. They should have made him look more dangerous, but, oddly, they didn't bother her. She knew he'd gotten them protecting people, just as he was protecting her right now. Obviously, he wasn't scared of stepping between his charge and a bullet.

That, actually, made her feel even safer when she was with him. "I think Philippe is coming over to talk to me. Maybe I can find out some information."

"Consider me already gone." Reese grabbed the bottle of lotion and rubbed some on, making it look like that was his only reason for stopping by. The man had some awesome muscles.

He was about to leave when Cavanaugh halted his progress, still a good twenty feet from them, and pulled a cell phone out of his pocket.

And then an odd thing happened. Philippe's whole body language changed. He went from king of the hill to subordinate in the split second it took to look at the LCD and identify the caller. His smarmy smile was gone. He was explaining something, growing frustrated, but holding it in check. He never once raised his voice.

Reese watched closely, too. "I wonder who the caller is." He nodded at the splendid compound. "Philippe is pretty high up. Can't be too many people out there who could make him kowtow like that."

"T?" she asked, using their code name for Tsernyakov.

"I think chances are good to excellent."

Sam looked away from Philippe, not wanting to get caught staring. The guy every law enforcement body in the world was searching for, the main target of their mission, was likely on the phone just a few yards away. If that was truly the case then she had gotten closer to him than anyone ever had before. And it was still light-years from pinpointing his location.

"What if we got the phone? Would that help?" she asked, suddenly inspired.

"Maybe, if we can get it to Brant Law and he can get it to a lab. Call records are not that easy to hide."

Her mind moved a mile a minute as she considered the possibility. "But how are we going swipe the phone?"

"Know anyone who has experience as a pickpocket?" Reese grinned at her, appearing all relaxed as if the key to all they sought hadn't just dropped into their laps.

He was right. They had a cover to keep. She took a slow breath and glanced back at Cavanaugh, who was putting away his cell.

Could she get it? So far, throughout the mission, she had the feeling that she was being overestimated. Yeah, her rap sheet was impressive, but that was only because she got caught practically every time she even thought about breaking the law. Brant, Nick and the women on her team thought her arrest record was the tip of the iceberg. But it had been nearly everything she'd done and some she hadn't. False representation.

Sure, she'd lifted a handful of wallets over the years from careless tourists. There were times when the shelters had been ruled by gangs at war with the one she had to stay loosely affiliated with to be allowed to hang out on the art museum side of Center City. No shelter access meant no food—except for Sundays when most churches had socials after service for those who attended, visitors invited. But by the following Wednesday, when she had already picked out every last crumb from her pockets, she did what was necessary to survive.

"Say we get the phone. How are we going to deflect suspicion?" she asked, pushing the past aside.

"Don't need to if he never realizes the phone is gone." Reese shrugged.

"A switch?"

"Why not? We'll let your team know, and they could have a replacement waiting for us. We'll go out on a WaveRunner ride later tonight and meet up with one of them."

"And if Philippe figures out the phone is gone while we're away?" She didn't like this plan. "An instant switch would be better."

Reese's eyes narrowed as he watched her. "You're right."

The simple admission thrilled her. "I get the make and model, we call it in to Brant. He gets a corrupted chip for it and gives it to us. Then I can switch the chips. We'll have Philippe's info, and he'll just think his phone broke."

Reese was grinning.

She couldn't help smiling back. His approval felt nice.

"Hope you are having fun." Cavanaugh finally reached them. "Sam." He nodded to her with a smile. "David," he greeted Reese.

"I'm going to take the boat out this morning." His attention was directed at Sam. "How about a little snorkeling? I know a spot that's near some rocky outcroppings. They block the current. There isn't much surge." He was back in gracious-host mode. All signs of the tension brought about by the phone call were gone.

"Absolutely," Sam said, although she could barely swim.

The important thing was that Cavanaugh would have to take the cell out of his pocket if he got into the water.

The man turned to Reese. "You are welcome, too, of course."

Reese gave him a level look. "Wouldn't miss it."

Cavanaugh's gaze hesitated on the scars on Reese's chest. "Law-school hazing that rough these days?"

"Not quite. College boys that stupid these days is more like it," he said as if disgusted with himself. "One too many beers at a frat party and I wrapped the car around the first phone pole. Learned my lesson." He even managed to look embarrassed. "It was a long time ago."

Cavanaugh nodded. "We all had our youthful digressions."

What was his? Sam watched him. Setting up a cocaine-distribution center on campus? "So do I need to bring anything?" she asked.

"I keep the equipment on the boat. Come as you are." Cavanaugh let his gaze run down the length of her as he offered her his arm.

She took it, despite the fact that having to touch him set her teeth on edge.

"I have to run back to the room to get something." Reese left them, probably so she could work her charm on Cavanaugh and get some information out of him.

The thought of having to get into the water—deep water with some really nasty fish in it, such as sharks, for example—had her mind buzzing, however, and they ended up talking about the dominant currents and the wind. Or rather, Cavanaugh talked and she pretended to understand. She knew little about the sea.

Four other people waited by the boat already, Eva entertaining them with one of her stories. Her boyfriend was nowhere in sight. They had a fairly loose sort of relationship that didn't exclude others. Good—the more distractions for Cavanaugh, the better. Reese caught up with them a few minutes later with a baseball cap for himself and one for her.

She tugged hers onto her head, wondering how long it would stay there once the boat picked up speed. "Thanks."

"Away we go, then." Cavanaugh grinned at his guests as he climbed in and got behind the wheel. As many possessions as he had, it seemed the man was still excited by his toys.

She made sure to stay near him and keep an eye on his pocket. If he took the phone out, she wanted to know where he put it.

He pulled away from shore abruptly, with a laugh, and the boat rattled on top of the waves. She grabbed the side and looked toward the sand they were rapidly leaving behind, not wanting to get fixated on all that open water ahead.

Once he'd made a point of admiring the electronics, Reese stood close beside her. "You okay?" He had to lean close to be heard over the noise of the motor.

His skin smelled coconutty from the suntan lotion he'd put on earlier. The look he gave her was neutral. Friendly.

What was that supposed to mean?

She was still confused by his reaction to their kiss the night before and hurt by his withdrawal afterward. Had she done something wrong? Granted, with her lack of experience she probably wasn't the world's best kisser. But this was it? He wasn't going to give her a second chance?

All that after she had given him the biggest compliment she had ever given, telling him that she felt safer with him than she had ever felt with a man. What more did he want?

"Yeah. I'm fine," she said and when her gaze dropped to his lips, she looked away. "I'm not a very strong swimmer. That's all."

"The water is calm."

"Can someone snorkel in a life vest?"

"I don't see why not."

"I'd better go and find one."

"Good idea." He was watching her as if he was trying to puzzle something out. "I'll stick close by once we go into the water. If you need to, just grab on to me."

She nodded her thanks, then wobbled toward the front of the boat in the hopes of spotting a vest.

Although the ocean was smooth, Cavanaugh was driving fast enough to make the ride interesting.

She found a seat nobody was using and lifted the top. Sure enough, there were three orange vests tucked in the box compartment. She grabbed the smallest just as Cavanaugh cut the motor and announced, "We are here."

She pulled the vest over her bikini and made sure the fastener was tight. Not that it made her feel any better. She glanced at Reese. He'd be close by. At least there was that.

"The ocean floor rises up here, so the water is not too deep. There's an old freight ship about twenty feet down. It sunk in a storm a good fifty years ago. You'll see lots of tropical fish around it. The goggles and snorkels are here." He pushed a large plastic crate forward with his feet. "Have fun, everyone."

Reese pulled out a mask and held it to her face. "Press on, then let go."

The mask fell off, and she grabbed for it.

"Not a good fit," he said. "When you press it to your face like that, it sticks if you have a good seal."

She tried another one, then another. The fourth seemed perfect.

The guests divvied up the equipment, but Cavanaugh made no move to take anything.

"You're not coming?" she asked him. How

were they going to get the phone away from him if he didn't let go of it?

"Somebody should probably stay with the boat," he said.

She thought for a moment then gave "the look" to Reese.

He ignored her.

She glared.

He shook his head slightly.

"Please," she mouthed when another guest said something to Cavanaugh and he turned his back to them.

Reese set his mouth in a thin line, but nodded after a second. "I could stay," he said. "Truth be told, I love boats, but I'm not that keen on being in the water."

Cavanaugh tilted his head, looking amused. "Is that so?"

"Since I've never done this before, I wouldn't mind having an expert's guidance." Sam tried to look lost and a little worried. It wasn't hard.

"Of course." Philippe pulled his shirt over his head and draped it on the back of the captain's chair. He had a body that clearly saw regular exercise, but it was still a far cry from Reese's. He reached into his swim shorts and pulled out the cell, then fiddled with something on the dashboard. A small compartment opened, into which he tossed the phone. After he'd closed the door, Sam noticed a tiny keypad.

He had a safe.

She was going to drown for nothing.

She shot a desperate look to Reese. He had a dark expression on his face and he looked as if he was about to step in and save her from Philippe and the water, but she shook her head slightly, pleading with him to stay put. Even if they couldn't get the phone, she might be able to get information out of Philippe while they were alone. She didn't have to like this. She just had to do it.

"Ready?" Philippe dug through the equipment and picked a green mask and flippers, put the latter on, then reached out a hand to help her to the edge of the boat from where she would have to jump.

Too late to change her mind now.

Here we go. She forced a smile, put on the goggles and splashed into the water. The glass fogged up almost immediately. She bobbed on the small waves, unable to see anything, grabbing for the strap.

"You didn't—" Philippe was right next to her. "Here. Take it off."

The vest kept her buoyant enough so she felt semisafe, despite the fact that even in the short minute or so they had already drifted away from the boat.

"This is what you have to do." Philippe spit into his mask. "Now rub it all over the optical surface then rinse it in the water. That should do."

Gross. She did it anyway.

"Let me help you with the mouthpiece."

Since he was reaching for it, she handed it over, thinking that it required a special trick, as well. But all he did was place it in her mouth while holding her gaze.

He probably meant it as a suggestive gesture. It felt plain creepy.

"Now put your head in the water and I'll adjust it for you."

She smiled as if she were having fun and did what he said.

Wow.

The water was clear enough to see the wreck below, covered with sea moss and shells. The small schools of colorful tropical fish that inhabited it were startling. Blue, green, yellow and silver scales flashed in the sunshine that filtered through the water. *Mesmerizing.*

Someone tapped her shoulder. She lifted her face out of the water and looked at Philippe, who was giving her the thumbs-up with a questioning expression.

He removed his mouthpiece. "How do you like it?"

"It's amazing," she said around hers and went back to watching.

Several minutes passed before her senses became filled enough with the enchantment to think of the phone. Could Reese pry the compartment open to get to it?

Not likely. She looked up just in time to see Eva climb back on board.

The woman was forever finagling a way to be near Reese. She was the most annoying of the guests. Just because she had the perfect body, it didn't mean she had to flash it every chance she got.

"Come on. I want to show you something else," Philippe said next to her.

Sam smiled at him and followed. She couldn't afford to look anything but enthusiastic about whatever he had to offer.

He went under, propelled by the fins he wore on his feet. She hadn't bothered to grab a pair of those since she wasn't going to take the vest off. He swam deeper, circled, then came up, blew the water out of his mouthpiece next to her.

She glanced back at the boat. Eva was practically sitting on Reese's lap. Maybe she should go back.

"This way," Philippe said.

She hesitated a second, then followed the man.

They swam the length of the ship and came to an odd rocklike formation, hard-looking but lacy at the same time, as if made from petrified tree branches.

"What is it?" she asked when both of their faces were out of the water.

"The beginnings of a coral reef."

She swam closer until she was on top of it and watched the fishes play. Philippe named a few and added some interesting tidbits about the wildlife down below, never missing an opportunity to brush against her when he went down to swim around and under her. She fixed an interested smile on her face and kept it there. They spent a good hour in the water before heading back.

"Anybody want to try another spot?" Philippe asked his guests once they were drinking cocktails on board. He had a minifridge under the console. The boat was a wonder.

"I want more," Eva said, looking straight at Reese.

More of what? Sam watched her. Eva had barely spent ten minutes in the water. So far, she'd spent most of her time with Reese.

If Eva kept getting in the way, she could mess things up. Sam needed to keep track of things that might have a bearing on their mission. It had nothing to do with jealousy.

"I'd love to go," she said. "But do you mind if I don't go in again?" She needed to stay on board and have a go at that keypad. Reese had no success with it, as he had indicated with a slight shake of his head when she had climbed back on board.

"Of course not." Philippe smiled. "It's your first time." He said the words with emphasis. "You need to get used to this. You can keep me company."

Her hopes wilted. Great.

The next good spot, according to Philippe, was just half a mile away. This time Eva did want to go in and insisted that Reese go with her. Sam and Philippe were the only two left on board.

"So how long is David staying on the island?" he asked. "I assume an important lawyer like him can't ignore work indefinitely."

"He's flying out next week. Probably." And that was the truth, something she didn't want to dwell on right now. She wouldn't have minded if Reese became a permanent member of the operation. Not because she enjoyed hanging out with him. He was good at what he did, that was all. He would have been an asset to any team.

Philippe seemed pleased with her response.

"You think—" The chirping of the cell phone interrupted him. He punched the code and retrieved the phone, looked at the display and decided to ignore the call, tossing the cell next to them on the seat—right on Sam's towel.

"Anyway, so back to David. He should check out

the Pirate Festival tomorrow. Some of the men are going out on a little tasting tour. There is usually a substantial display of Caribbean rum. I believe the ladies are staying on the beach. The festival has a tendency to get rowdy as the day wears on."

Was that an attempt to get rid of Reese for a while? "Sounds like fun. He'll probably want to check that out," she said, playing along.

Philippe leaned closer. "Perhaps—"

Once again, he didn't get to finish. Gretchen LaSalle, a leggy blonde, was coming up from the water, her hand bleeding. "Moray eel bit me," she said much more calmly than Sam would have.

Cavanaugh moved for the first-aid kit. Gretchen's attention was on the hand that dripped blood down her leg. Sam grabbed the cell phone and flipped it over.

Come on, come on, come on. She stuck a fingernail under the release and popped off the back, keeping an eye on the other two in the boat. *Don't look, don't look, don't look.*

Philippe was turning just as she finally got the chip out. She shoved it in the waistband of her bikini, pretending to adjust it with one hand while grabbing for her towel with the other. She hadn't had a chance to put the back of the phone in place. It lay there in pieces. Cavanaugh hadn't seen it yet.

"What can I do to help?" She snapped the towel

off the seat so the movement tossed the phone over the side of the boat. It entered the water with a splash.

Philippe glanced back at the sound.

She did her best to look stricken. "Your phone!" She rushed to bend over the side. The silver gadget was sinking. "I'm so sorry. Can we get it back?"

She turned around and held her breath, waiting for his reaction, watching for any hint that he was on to her. Had he seen, maybe in his peripheral vision, what she had done? Or was he buying the act?

He watched her for a long second.

What if he *had* seen her? Did he have a gun on board? Knowing the kind of things he was involved in, he probably had ten. If she screamed, would Reese hear her? Could he get to the boat in time? If he did, what could he do?

An annoyed expression flashed across Philippe's face, but it was gone in a second. "Never mind. The phone is nothing." He was bringing the kit over the next second.

Was he letting this go in front of Gretchen and planning to get her later? Sam kept an eye on him, desperate to gauge his mood and possible intentions. He seemed completely focused on the task at hand. How good an actor was he? Had to be pretty good to be as successful as he was in business.

She wrapped the towel around Gretchen's

shoulders then grabbed a bottle of mineral water. "Let's rinse." She did that while looking to Philippe again. "I'm really sorry. I just panicked from the blood." She didn't have any trouble making her voice sound like she was all shook up.

He considered her for a second. "I have other phones. No big deal. Let's take care of Gretchen." He really seemed pretty nice about it, considering that it had been an expensive-looking model. He got out the disinfectant and poured it over the wound then dabbed it with a piece of gauze.

"It's not that bad now that I'm looking at it." Gretchen inspected the wound. "In the water, I couldn't tell how serious it was."

"Could you hold this?" Philippe handed Sam a pair of scissors. He wrapped the wound up tight, using a whole roll of bandage. "I'll blow the horn and get everyone to come in, then we can head back to shore."

Gretchen flexed her hand. "I don't think that's necessary."

But another guest was already pulling himself over the edge of the boat. He took in the first-aid kit. Brian Wallace. Sam made a point to memorize every guest's name so she could pass them on to Brant Law.

"What happened? I saw her swimming in like there was trouble."

Gretchen explained. One more reason to stay out of the water.

Sam glanced at Philippe, who was being a very solicitous host to Gretchen, making her a drink. The other guests were coming in, as well. They'd probably seen that some had made it to the boat already. Eva and Reese returned last—a good fifteen minutes after the others—laughing. Had a good time out there, did they?

And why was that surprising? Reese was a normal guy; he deserved a normal, emotionally healthy woman who wasn't bound by the filth of her past.

Reese will leave soon.

It didn't matter, Sam told herself. He had already given her so much, and for that she would be forever grateful. He had made her realize that not all men were cruel, that she wasn't doomed to be bound by her fears and memories, that there was a chance to move on. He had watched her back and helped her to do her part in the operation. With his assistance, the week at Cavanaugh's mansion might end up a success instead of a disaster. And she *had* enjoyed that kiss.

But she was going to ignore all the weird things he made her feel. The mission was the important thing.

And she had Cavanaugh's cell chip with a call record that might finally point them to Tsernyakov.

Chapter Six

Reese stared at the ceiling, listening to Sam's soft breathing next to him, watching her outline in the dark. She was so far over, if she leaned a smidgen, she would fall to the floor. He made a point to always keep the distance she set, not wanting to make her feel any more uncomfortable than she already was.

They'd decided against taking the WaveRunner out in the night, as Philippe's men had seemed to set up night surveillance. Did they think the kid might still be hiding somewhere on the property? Sam had suggested that they could hook up with Brant at the festival the next day. He'd agreed. The few hours they would have gained by making the drop-off tonight weren't worth the risk.

He closed his eyes, willing sleep to come. That seemed unlikely, just as it had since they'd been sharing a bed. And when he did sleep, it was the usual nightmares, fighting bad guys, searching the darkness for the people he was supposed to save. Natalie.

A small sound coming from Sam made his eyes pop open again. She moved her head a fraction, and he could see in the moonlight that her eyes were moving rapidly under the lids. She was dreaming. Her face scrunched up. Dreaming something bad?

He watched her, wanting to put a soothing arm around her, but not wanting to scare her even more. She would likely think it a restraint instead of a soothing gesture, turning her nightmare worse still.

Then she opened her mouth and a single hoarse cry broke loose. "No!" she said in a child's voice, so poignant it gripped his heart and wouldn't let go.

He swore under his breath, moved closer and pulled her into his arms. "Shh. You're safe. Nobody is going to hurt you now," he whispered.

For a split second she bowed her body, resisting, then her face fell against his bicep and she inhaled deeply and the next moment, without warning, snuggled into him. He held still. Did she recognize his scent? Did she, after the last couple of days with him, associate him with safety as she had claimed? As much as he hadn't been able to appreciate her declaration after their mind-blowing kiss, now the thought caused his heart to thump in an odd rhythm.

If this was what she needed, he would happily hold her all night. He wasn't going to sleep, anyway.

But after a few moments, his eyes did drift closed and, comforted by her even breathing, he fell into a deep, dreamless sleep, the kind he rarely experienced.

In the morning, waking before she did, he pulled away reluctantly, knowing that waking in his arms would make her feel instantly uncomfortable by the light of day. He was in the shower by the time he heard her move around, making coffee in the kitchen.

THE PIRATE FESTIVAL WAS about as chaotic as a pirate attack must have been back in the day—too many jostling people who smelled like rum, and constant screaming, in this case coming from the rides.

"I should have stayed on the beach," Sam said, and paused in front of a cotton-candy stand. Her eyes rounded and her tongue darted out to lick the corners of her lips.

She looked like a little kid. At least, her expression did. The rest of her was dressed for a "date." Her black pants molded to her curves, as did the silver-gray tank top. She had on heels and with that she was nearly at eye level with Reese. He couldn't resist those eyes.

"What flavor?" Reese stepped in line behind a young boy who was handing over a fistful of change to the vendor.

"Berry. But you don't have to buy me one. I have my own money." She reached toward her back pocket.

He simply shrugged, made his purchase then handed over the stick.

"Thanks." She pinched off a fist-size chunk and practically inhaled it, just about moaned as the sweetness melted on her tongue. She licked her fingers, too.

He pressed his lips together hard enough to hurt.

"Want some?" She was grinning with pleasure.

He wanted plenty, but shook his head and tried to focus on the candy. "So what are we talking about here? Addiction or just a serious weakness?"

She smiled at him. "Permanent character flaw."

Her kidlike response to the festival was fun to watch, very different from the wary, defensive stance she assumed most of the time. Steel-band music filled the air. The aroma of meat roasting over open pits and the dizzying colors of the Pirate Festival enveloped them. Sam kept at her cotton candy as they walked.

"Have you seen Brant yet?" she asked between two mouthfuls.

She had incredible lips. Incredible everything really, and yeah, he'd spent the last few months out in the field, but he'd done that before and still hadn't been affected like this by any woman upon his return. And yet it wasn't the physical attraction that made him nervous. He could, would, deal with that. But there were other undertones, a kind of pull that he felt toward her more and more each day.

She was incredibly tough, hurt in the past and yet still hopeful, giving one hundred percent to get the job done. For the past hour, as they'd walked around, he watched her wide-eyed enjoyment of the fair. He'd also been thinking about other places in the world he would love to show her. He was an idiot.

"What is it?" She was looking at him.

What were they talking about? Brant. "A few minutes ago."

"Why isn't he coming over?"

"Cavanaugh's man is still behind us."

To her credit, she didn't turn around. "Do you think Philippe is on to us?"

The same question popped up over and over in his head since they had left their host's mansion that morning and he had picked up on the tail. He could have easily lost Roberto, but that would have made them look even more suspicious. They had to act out the lovers-out-on-the-town charade until the guy decided there was nothing more to them and went back home.

It could take a while. He found he didn't mind much.

"I shouldn't have come," Sam repeated and licked the empty stick, looking more contented than he'd ever seen her.

"I didn't think it was a good idea to leave you alone with Cavanaugh for hours on end. If he pressed you into something you didn't want to do—" He still couldn't put the picture of Cavanaugh touching Sam on the beach out of his mind. And, of course, Cavanaugh had stayed back at the mansion, since he'd seen the festival dozens of times. A number of his guests attended, however. Reese caught glimpses of them from time to time in the crowd and avoided them. He wanted to make sure Sam and he were alone so they could meet Brant when he showed up. He'd called the guy as soon as they'd cleared Philippe's gates.

"I could outmaneuver him." She tossed the stick into the nearest garbage receptacle. "Probably."

It was that *probably* he'd been worried about. "You're sure he didn't see when you handled his phone?"

"Pretty sure. His back was turned." She was staring up at a giant Ferris wheel. There was that longing look on her face again.

"Let's go for a ride," he said on impulse.

"Really?" Her slow grin spread from ear to ear. "I haven't been on one of these since…forever."

Yeah. He'd figured that. Walking through the festival with her made it painfully clear just how different her childhood had been from his—an all-American boy growing up in an all-American neighborhood living the all-American life that included two trips to Disneyland.

Thinking about her past had his stomach in a hard ball every time. He found it difficult to accept that there was nothing he could do about it.

An older gentleman carrying an armful of roses walked up to them as they stood in line for the ride. "A flower for the beautiful lady?"

Why not? Reese pulled some money out of his pocket and picked the nicest bloom.

The tops of her cheeks tinged with pink. "You shouldn't do all this," she said, but her eyes were gleaming as she accepted the rose.

And out of the blue, he felt as embarrassed as she looked. What on earth was he doing here, wooing her?

Not wooing. Not wooing at all, he assured

himself and almost believed it. "We are being watched," he said. "This is how a man acts when he's in love with a woman."

Her eyes went wide. She looked as if she was about to lose her smile, but then she turned from him to slip into the seat the attendant was holding still for them, and he could no longer see her expression.

He got in next to her. The wheel turned so the next couple could get in. Cavanaugh's man watched from a distance. Didn't look as though he had any intention of joining them. Maybe Roberto didn't like rides. Good to know.

He was the guy who had brought the kid into the boathouse the night before. What was he doing following them? Reese was a hundred percent sure they hadn't been seen that night, had made sure.

They went up another level, then another. Then the ride was full and the attendant started up the motor. Reese looked out over the beach as they climbed higher and higher. It had been a while for him, too.

"Isn't it awesome?" Sam was smiling again.

He took her hand, although he wasn't sure if Cavanaugh's man could see the gesture. Still, it couldn't hurt for them to stay in character.

She must have thought the same thing because she leaned against him.

"So how did you become a professional body-guard? Why aren't you a lawyer like David? Aren't twins supposed to do everything together?"

He looked over at her and raised an eyebrow. "Have you been talking to my mother?" He'd heard the why-can't-you-be-a-lawyer-like-your-brother-and-stop-risking-your-life question all too often in the past.

She smiled at him, and her beauty took his breath away.

"So you were never interested in law?" she asked.

"We went to law school together." He didn't want to think about those memories.

"What happened?"

Natalie. "Things didn't work out and I left. I joined the army."

"You had a big fight over some girl. His wife?" Her eyes widened. She was clearly enjoying putting together some big tragic romance, broken hearts and all that. "You're still in love with her?"

"Life is not like the romance movie of the week on the Hallmark Channel." His own good mood was evaporating fast.

She seemed to pick up on that. "I'm sorry. It's none of my business." She pulled away.

He missed her warmth. He needed it against the memories. "Her name was Natalie," he said and pulled Sam back against him.

"What happened to her?"

He didn't think he could say the words, but they came out, if a little weak. "She was raped."

She sucked in a sharp breath and tightened her arms around him. How strange that was, that a woman who could accept no physical comfort from another person was now comforting him, the man who was supposed to protect *her?*

The gesture loosened something inside him. "We were out with the team—I played football." And hadn't touched one since. "She had a headache and decided to go home. Instead of going with her, I stayed with the guys. I needed to blow off some steam. Was going to go after her in an hour or so. I was too late. Some creep got her in the parking lot of her apartment building."

"It wasn't your fault," she said fiercely.

"Wasn't it?" How could she forgive him so easily, when someone had done the same thing to her, let people hurt her? Why wasn't she mad at the world, at him who had done the same to another?

"What happened to her?" she asked.

His throat tightened. "She was in a car accident a few weeks later and died." He remembered the afternoon clearly. Natalie wouldn't talk to him, had shut him out completely. She was drinking. He could hear it in her voice over the phone. He went over to her place anyway. She was already gone. Later, when he was told what had happened, he was never sure if she had crossed over into the oncoming lane on purpose or by accident.

"I didn't attend classes for a good month after that. Then I left."

"And spent your life saving others ever since to make up for it?"

He thought for a second. "It wasn't like that. I'm not that heroic. I fell into the job. After the army I was offered a position as a security expert for a global company. Then, when the CEO was traveling to a tough overseas location on business, he decided to take me as a sort of bodyguard. There were a couple of altercations. I handled them. Word got out in his circle. I got other offers."

She didn't look convinced. She did look somber, however, and he regretted that. She'd been having a good time until he'd dumped his past on her. And she was due a few lighthearted moments. He wasn't going to take that away from her.

The wheel went around and around, showing them a breathtaking view of the cavalcade on the beach, the ocean and the private yachts rocking on the waves, the impressive skyline of the city. She was still pressed against him, and he felt relaxed suddenly, as if the weight of his past regrets had been lightened by having her listen to him.

"It's beautiful up here," she whispered, apparently losing herself to the sights again.

Good. "We have plenty of time. We can try whatever you want."

She smiled and some old shadows disappeared from around his heart. He wasn't prepared to examine how much of that came from having her snuggled into him. He wanted to touch his lips to hers and seek total oblivion there.

He looked away.

He couldn't think like that. She felt comfortable with him, and he fully realized what a big deal that was for her. He wasn't going to ruin that by making some stupid move again. That wasn't what she needed.

She didn't need another person in her life who would eventually let her down, and with him that was a given. He couldn't give her what she needed, a stable family of her own at last, a man who loved her and would protect her and was a steady presence in her life day in and day out. She'd been let down by her mother, by her stepfather, by the system, foster parents, everyone. He'd be damned if he'd join that list. He had a job that took him out of the country eight to ten months of the year. She needed someone who would stand by her.

He shouldn't have kissed her in the first place. What had he been thinking?

That kissing her would be nice.

And, unfortunately, it had gone way beyond that. Nice didn't begin to describe the heat of desire that had sliced through him when their lips met. Might as well forget all about it because it wasn't going to happen again. *Absolutely not. Never.*

"You okay?" he asked to distract himself.

But the question made her look up at him, putting her mouth just inches from his. *Way to go.*

"When it stops, can we stay on and go one more time?" She was lit from within with excitement.

He scratched his lips, which were pulling into a grin. This much, at least, he could do for her. "Sure we can."

So they did the Ferris wheel again, then some nasty ride called Honduras Hurricane. Once again, Cavanaugh's man stayed on the ground. When they stood in line for bungee jumping—did he agree to that?—Reese signaled to Brant. He climbed up onto the tower right behind them.

"Are you sure?" Reese asked Sam as they were getting strapped into the harness for a tandem jump. "We can still step back." *Not that he was scared.*

"I always wanted to try." She was practically vibrating with anticipation.

Reese took a deep breath.

Brant made a show of looking over the railing. "I might just change my mind," he said to the family of four behind him.

"It's up to you, sir." The assistant shrugged with a superior expression on his overtanned face.

Brant's hand hesitated over the consent form. Reese flashed him an I-dare-you look. He glared at him as he signed.

"Wait." Reese took his baseball cap off and handed it to him. "Could you please hold on to this for me?"

"Sure." He bit the word out with as much displeasure as could be squeezed into one syllable.

Reese watched as he ran his finger along the cap's trim and his thumb paused on the chip inside. Goal accomplished. They had made dropoff. Now it was up to the rest of the team to break through the protective layers and get to the information hidden in the circuits. From what he'd heard about Carly, the resident hacker on the team, whatever encryption was used didn't stand a chance.

"Okay. Hold on to each other," the assistant told him and smiled at Sam.

Men always smiled at her. Not that she let it go to her head. If anything, it seemed to make her uncomfortable.

Reese glanced down then decided it would be

better if he didn't focus on the drop. How on earth had she talked him into jumping off a two-hundred-foot-tall crane? Maybe the Ferris wheel had scrambled his brain. The distance looked even greater from above than it had from below. He should have stopped by the rum-tasting tent first.

"I have to say, the distance doesn't feel right to me."

"Too long?" she teased with a raised eyebrow.

"Too short. Even if we had a parachute it wouldn't open."

"You've parachuted before?" She seemed surprised by this.

Maybe it seemed unlikely, given his current reluctance. "I was a trainer," he said and shifted as the assistant adjusted the harness between his legs.

Who on earth had come up with this insane idea for entertainment?

"No worries about anything opening or not here." Sam looked up at him.

Brant was grinning behind them. *Your time is coming, buddy.* Reese tossed him a hard look then turned back to Sam.

"We don't have a parachute," she was saying.

"Thanks." He would have trusted something he was familiar with and had checked, rechecked and packed himself.

"Anytime you're ready." The assistant tugged

the harness one last time to check for snugness. "Don't forget to yell *bungee* as you go."

Sam grinned into Reese's eyes. "One, two, three." She pulled him over the edge. "BUNGEE!!!"

He yelled a word that wasn't as clean as that.

As he descended, though, he began to enjoy it. A hundred and fifty feet of free fall with Sam holding on to him for dear life. They were pressed as closely together as possible. The cord reached its full length but actually accelerated instead of slowing down as it went into the stretch. Then they reached the end point and catapulted back up.

Sam was laughing, just peals of laughter, as they bounced back and forth.

He held her tight, not wanting the ride to end.

By the time it did, his brain cells felt scrambled. The first thing he saw when he could take his eyes off Sam and focus on his surroundings was Cavanaugh's man watching them with a bored expression. The second was the kid from the boathouse a few feet behind him. Neither had seen the other one yet.

"Wasn't that great?" Sam asked as they were being pulled back up. She had a permanent grin on her face.

"A worthwhile experience." But despite it all, he said, "Let's not do it again."

When they were back on the platform, harness

free, he thanked Brant for holding his cap and took it back. The chip was no longer inside.

He bent next to him to fix his shoes. "Sixteen-year-old, green shorts, striped shirt, right next to the jewelry stand. Grab him if you can," he said so low he wasn't sure whether or not Brant had heard him.

But the FBI agent said, "Sorry. Changed my mind. Just can't do it." And stepped out of the harness the assistant was snapping on him. Then he was out of there and going down the stairs.

"Scared the big guy, did we?" The assistant sneered. "Who's next?"

Reese grabbed Sam's hand and pulled her after him. No time for gawking. "We have to distract our tail and give Brant a chance," he said and, once they were out of hearing distance of the others, explained what he had seen while hanging from the cord and what he thought should be done about it.

"Why take the kid?" Sam followed, picking up on his sense of urgency.

"He might have enough information on Cavanaugh to lock him up for good once we have Tsernyakov and we no longer need the man."

"You think he'll talk?"

"He might. And whatever happens, he will be better off in custody than on the streets, hunted by Cavanaugh's men. The island is not that big. His luck is bound to run out."

She looked as if she was mulling that over. "You think maybe Brant could do something for him? Like put him in a rehab program for juveniles or something? You know, back in the States."

"We'll talk to him about it," he said.

They were near enough to see Brant closing in on the kid, who was staring at the jumpers and slurping some kind of soft drink from a plastic cup. He was now right behind Cavanaugh's man, still not recognizing the danger he was in.

Reese squeezed Sam's hand, pointed in the opposite direction. "Run!" he said and took off at full speed, dodging the crowd, making sure she stayed close behind. He didn't stop until they were a good three hundred feet down the beach where stilt walkers entertained the crowd, then stared at them as if watching the performers had been the sole reason for their hurry.

Roberto arrived behind them and came so close this time, they could hear him huffing. And all of a sudden, Reese was fed up with the man. What did he want from them, anyway?

"Ready for some fun?" he asked Sam.

She gave him a puzzled look and glanced between the stilt walkers and him. "You want to try?"

"Not that." He grinned. Frankly, he was still a little dizzy from the jump. "Let's have some fun with our faithful *friend*."

He turned and looked right at Cavanaugh's man, put a surprised smile on his face. "Hey, haven't I seen you around Philippe Cavanaugh's place? You're a friend of his?"

SAM WATCHED as the burly, well over six-foot-tall guy turned ruddy in the cheeks.

"Uh…" he said then repeated it. "Just looking for my buddy. Have fun." He turned on his heels and lumbered away.

Sam grinned at the man's retreat then reminded herself that the guy was far from harmless. He'd been ready to kill a sixteen-year-old hustler the other night. "Don't you think Cavanaugh will be suspicious that we recognized his man? If he figures we're checking to see whether we are being followed, he'll think we have something to hide."

"I wouldn't worry about it. I don't think Bubba here will be bragging about his incompetence. Cavanaugh doesn't strike me as a man who easily forgives mistakes."

He was probably right.

"Would you like to go back to the mansion or walk around here a little more?" he asked.

She'd enjoyed the festival. Spending time with Reese was nice. More than nice, making her wish…she wasn't sure what. He had shown a different, more carefree side than usual. She wouldn't have minded seeing more of it.

But they had work to do.

Chapter Seven

That night there was a bonfire party arranged by
Philippe so his guests could view the fireworks the
city put on for the festival.

Eva chatted incessantly, having had too much
rum punch. She entertained them with horror
stories from her line of work as a Realtor.

"And then we go in. And right there on the
living-room floor is the owner going at it like crazy
with a woman in the most awful, gaudy domina-
trix outfit. So my client just falls on them, shouting
and swearing, grabs the whip and beats them like
a madman. It turns out the woman is his wife. He
was looking to buy her the beachfront condo as an
anniversary gift."

Her audience laughed with her. "No, no, that's
not the worst part. So then this strange calm comes
over the guy and he grabs me and says if the wife

could do it then so can he. We should all four of us have fun together."

"So did you do it?" One of the guys shouted out the question from the other side of the fire.

"You pig," Eva admonished him. But then she put on a mysterious smile. "A lady doesn't kiss and tell." And laughed at the applause and hooting that she got.

"You have an interesting line of work," Reese remarked quietly as someone started into another story.

Eva had somehow found a way to sit on his other side. "It's fun. Especially now." She took another sip of her drink.

"Business is booming?" he asked nonchalantly.

Sam was looking at the current storyteller but was listening for Eva's answer.

"Now that Philippe is booming," she said.

"Right," he agreed as if he knew all about it. "He's extending his empire again."

Several weeks ago, Anita had followed Philippe to a private meeting at the Chamber of Commerce Charity Ball and overheard a discussion about a real-estate deal. The team hadn't been able to turn up more information about that yet, weren't sure if the deal was in any way tied to Tsernyakov.

"He's obsessed with that island, isn't he? I don't see the attraction. It's small and flat. *Boo-ring.*" She pressed a finger over her lips and smiled.

"Don't tell anyone I said that. The locals are fiercely proud. Okay, so it has some good diving, but who wants to be underwater all the time?"

What island? Sam leaned closer without being too obvious about it. Was Cavanaugh trying to buy a whole island? Could someone do that?

"You think he'll succeed?" Reese asked.

"Not much stands in his way when he decides he wants something." A hint of bitterness crept into Eva's voice. But then she brightened. "Keeps my bills paid and then some. Commission is nice and it's not about to end. He owns less than a tenth of available land. There are still a hundred owners left that he could buy out."

"You think he'll get it all?"

Eva glanced at him with a slight flicker of annoyance. "Not all of it, of course. Not the parts owned by the government. But the others." She shrugged. "They might sell eventually. Everybody has a price. And—"

"What are you whispering about over there?" Philippe called to her. "If you have any more saucy stories, let's hear them. Do be fair, *ma chérie*." He grinned.

Eva sobered and pulled back—she'd been leaning toward Reese. She set her glass on the sand. "I think I've had enough *sauce* for one night."

Philippe laughed. "Why don't you tell us about how you were stranded in a villa for two days with a client waiting out Hurricane Ivan?"

But Eva didn't get to tell that tale. The fireworks started and drowned out everything else as stars showered from the night sky above. The extravagant display went on for a solid hour. The party continued for another three hours after that, but Eva didn't return to her topic.

Around midnight, the group of guests began breaking up. By the end, only Reese, Sam, Eva and Philippe remained.

"Let's take a stroll before we call it a night." Reese stood and extended a hand toward Sam. When they were out of hearing distance, he said, "I'm hoping Philippe will go to bed by the time we get back and we might talk to Eva while she's willing."

She nodded. By morning the woman would be sober and might realize she'd said more than she should have.

Sam walked along the surf, not minding when an errant wave washed over her feet now and then. She loved the sound of the ocean. It seemed to carry the spirit of infinite peace.

Six months ago, she would have thought it unimaginable that she would ever get to see a place like this, would ever be walking in the moonlight with a man like Reese. He was a revelation when it came to men. He was strong but never abused his strength. He was honorable, gentle, funny, but could be serious, too, when the situation called for it.

She was starting to think that the world wasn't a completely horrible place to live in. Not if it had men like Reese in it and women like Anita and Gina and Carly. It amazed her how unconditionally and completely they'd accepted her from the beginning.

And if they had, knowing her record and all that, could others do the same? Did she really have a chance at a normal future? For a normal relationship even? She glanced at Reese.

He was watching her. "What are you thinking about?" he asked as he took her hand.

She wasn't about to reveal that she'd been thinking about him. And, dear God, she had been thinking about him a lot lately. Which was natural. Completely natural, she told herself. They were together twenty-four hours a day. Not noticing him would have been impossible. She needed to change the subject.

"What island do you think Eva was talking about?"

"My guess would be Little Cayman. It has less than two hundred permanent residents. It's small and flat. There is an antique map of the island behind the couch in Cavanaugh's living room. I saw it when I came to get you the other day."

"Why does he need it?"

"It's out of sight. He conducts his business here in plain view of his neighbors. He has to sneak around. Even if he manages to own fifty percent or so of the real estate on the island, do you realize what kind of power that would give him?"

Not really. She could barely imagine owning any property, let alone an island or even a small portion of one. "You think he wants to break in to the next level?" And what was the next level, anyway?

Reese considered that. "If he does, the power struggle will be something to watch. Illegal drugs and weapons and human trafficking are not virgin territories. For him to get bigger, he has to take from someone else. At a level that high, we are not talking about amateurs. Some of these people have their own private armies."

They walked in silence for a while, reached the end of the property then turned back. The bonfire had died down. Both Philippe and Eva were gone. Had they retired for the night together?

Sam let her gaze glide along the shoreline. She could see the lights of the Ferris wheel down the beach. It was no longer turning.

"Thank you for everything this morning. I had fun."

He grinned at her. "Me, too. You're fearless, you know that?"

Hardly. But it was nice to hear.

"Ever thought about extreme sports?"

She hadn't thought about sports at all. Ever since she could remember, all she thought about was survival. But things were different now. She had a job. She had some money collecting in the bank. She hadn't really spent any of it other than for basic necessities. Truth be told, she wasn't comfortable with it.

"I'm thinking about extreme living," she said.

He grinned. "Good. You're due for some fun. What are you going to do when this mission is over?"

"Probably stay on the island. I like this place." She looked away. "I have nothing to go back to." Something caught her eye on the sand and she bent to pick it up. Sea glass. Blue. Those were rare. She kept it. "I want to learn. Maybe go to school."

She had her GED, had gotten it during one of those times when she had spent a few months with a foster family before running away again. The Bakers had been okay. She wondered what they were doing now. They'd been the most decent of the bunch, but by then she was too scarred to fit in anywhere.

Back then she used to believe that she didn't deserve anything good. The prison shrink and the other women on the team had had considerable influence over her since then. Now she could almost believe that some measure of happiness was possible.

Especially at times like this when she was walking along a moonlit beach with Reese.

He had kissed her.

What did that mean?

What do you think it means, Sherlock? a voice dripping with sarcasm asked in her head. Her old voice. *What do you think he wants? What do men always want?*

She shook her head. Reese wasn't like that. He had never tried to push her into anything.

Could he want someone like her? Knowing what he knew about her past?

He'd kissed me once. The voice of hope spoke up.

She trusted Reese. If she couldn't make it with him, she couldn't make it with anyone.

She stopped and faced him.

"What is it?" he asked, his expression attentive.

Everything. Her new life was strange and overwhelming in ways she wasn't used to.

And Reese…

She was trusting him way too fast, growing to like him even faster. She was coming to rely on him to be there and back her up when she was in a bind. Which was okay, while they were here—

that was the idea behind their partnership. But she had to be very, very careful not to grow used to it, not to sink into some unreasonable fantasy that this might continue beyond the job.

Because he would never want that. Would he?

She was too chicken to talk. Instead, she rose to the tips of her toes and pressed her lips to his.

EVEN FIRST KISSES weren't as sweet as this one. Reese could barely remember his—at twelve with a girl of thirteen who lived down the street. Hell, he could barely remember anything with Sam's lips pressed against his with all the hopeful innocence that lived in the woman. It was a miracle that she had that despite her past. She had overcome.

He was proud of her for that. Admired her inner strength and spirit.

And despite knowing full well that this wasn't the smartest thing to do, he kissed her back.

She pressed against him with a soft little sigh that came from inside the hard shell she had woven around herself for protection. And that small sound melted his heart.

He knew all about shells. He hadn't taken his protective shield off in nearly a decade. He wasn't going to now. He was just going to taste her a little longer. Something to take back into the fight with him when he left.

For the most, he scared women—decent women he could have someday down the road imagined a relationship with. They didn't want a man who got calls in the middle of the night and left for months at a time, doing what he did when he was away. He had killed men. Not just one or two.

Then there were the women who were thrilled by this, who wanted him to talk about it, who were in love with the idea of some macho hero he was not. His occasional, very temporary liaisons tended to come from this group. Nobody went too deep. Nobody expected much. Nobody got hurt.

And now here was Sam, a woman he could not classify, one of a kind.

Kissing her was as close to heaven as he figured he would ever come. He ran a finger down her slender arms and pulled her to him. They fit each other to perfection. Knowing that, wanting her despite his better judgment, had been killing him for the last few days. He had to walk away. But he wasn't ready to let her go, not yet. He wanted a little more of her. Soon enough, she would push him away anyway.

And the reason behind that, her past, drove him to fury. He gentled his touch even more. He would have given his life to protect her. But that wasn't what she needed. She didn't need another shield.

She needed to heal from the past and be able to move away from it, to grow strong enough to be able to live freely, out in the open. And she had it in her. She was that strong. He would have given anything to be able to be there as that happened.

"I love your hair," he murmured into her ear before he kissed the soft spot below it. He tugged on a curl, let the silk slip through his fingers.

She sounded distracted when she spoke. "It used to be black."

So David had told him. "You're perfect as you are."

He ran his hands down her slim back then up again, soaking in the feel of her in his arms. He wanted badly to move forward and cup her breasts—he was a man, not a saint—but wasn't sure if he would scare her if he tried. He didn't want to push. More than anything, he wanted her to be able to enjoy what was happening between them.

But his hands crept toward their desired destination of their own volition. Okay. He'd stop the second he felt her stiffen. He could beat a hasty retreat in the blink of an eye.

But when his palms got there, instead of pulling away, she pressed her body into them.

Heaven help him.

He had to snap out of it. Do something to stop

this before they got carried away. He grabbed hold of her hand and dragged her into the waves.

"What are you doing?" she squealed.

He grinned. "Cooling off."

They were in deep enough so a larger wave lifted them both off their feet. She wrapped her arms around his neck and clung to him.

"Relax," he said, and wished he could take his own advice. Having her body pressed to his did nothing to assuage the fever of desire that coursed through his body and drew every muscle taut.

"I'm not a good swimmer."

"Can you trust me?"

She looked at him for a long moment. "I'll try."

He glanced up and down the beach and found a spot where the waves weren't breaking as hard as where they stood. "Hang on to my neck." He swam for it.

She trusted him enough, at least, to do that.

"Okay. Turn on your back. I'll hold you up," he said when they reached the spot he'd been aiming for.

She hesitated. "I can't float. I tried before."

"I'm not going to let you go."

She flipped onto her back and stretched her body on top of the water, her eyes clearly saying she didn't expect this to work.

He placed both hands under her back. "Relax."

Her flat, bare stomach and her delectable bikini-clad breasts were inches from his face, as if her body were being served to him on a platter by the ocean. And God help him, he wanted a taste more than he'd ever wanted anything in life.

"Don't think about sinking. Don't think about this at all. Picture yourself relaxing on the soft sand on the beach. You're safe, languid, breathing regularly."

He loosened his hold on her a fraction to see if she could hold herself on top of the water on her own. She felt the change and tightened her muscles, her body going rigid, which, of course, made her start to sink.

"Don't let me go."

"Not until you're ready."

Half an hour passed before they got to that point.

"I did it!" She clamped her arms around his neck, grinning with triumph. "Thanks."

His body went hard from the contact all over again. So much for cooling off in the water. "That was all you. I didn't do anything. Feeling more comfortable in the water?"

"Much."

"Now about the swimming part—" He needed to put a little distance between them.

"Tonight?" She disengaged her arms and treaded water.

"Here's the thing. You know how to swim, the basics, anyway. To become a stronger swimmer, all you have to do is practice. So let's do it. Parallel to shore. We'll go side by side. When you get tired, you let me know and you can rest. I'll hold you up."

The exercise would do him good, too, sap some of the excess energy that was humming through his body from her nearness.

The swimming part went well, actually. Him holding her in the water in his arms while she rested, however, undid his tenuous hold on self-control every single time.

He was grateful when she finally said, "Okay, I think I'm done. Let's call it a night."

He let her walk out of the water in front of him so she wouldn't see the silhouette of his swimming shorts in the moonlight and realize the shape he was in. *She* was in fabulous shape, water running down her sinuous body, pearls of it rolling off her tempting curves.

She threw herself onto the sand and stared up at the sky. He sat next to her and pulled up his legs, wrapped his arms around his knees.

"Thanks again," she said.

"No big deal. You should practice. If you're going to spend time near water on this mission, you should get good at swimming."

"Yes, sir."

"You're mocking me?" He looked over and his breath caught in his throat.

"Who, me?" she asked with a mischievous glint in her eyes.

She looked stunning when she was lighthearted like this, without the usual shadows in her gaze. Irresistible. He lowered his head, as though being drawn to a magnet. Her eyes widened as he touched his lips to hers.

Desire shot through him, hot and hard, making his body taut with need and his mind reel. He kissed her with reverence, barely daring to hold her, worried about scaring her. He recognized every second for the gift that it was and drank her in until he was drunk with the feel of her. He pulled away, breathing hard, grappling for control.

Now would be a good time to stop.

But she glanced up at him with what looked a lot like desire in the light of the moon and that undid him all over again.

He reached for her bikini top. He needed to feel the velvet of her skin without the fabric between them. He needed one taste. That would be it. That was as far as he would go.

She put a hand on his. *Not yet, don't make me stop yet,* a part of him protested, while the rest of him breathed in relief. Everything was getting out of control so fast. It was good that she stopped him now. He didn't want to hurt her. He looked up into her face. "Sorry. You're okay?"

She didn't respond, but lifted her lips to his again. Then she moved her hand up his arm to embrace him.

Desire thrilled through him, sharp and hot. And he knew half measures were never going to be enough. That it was going to kill him to let her go. But it was too late now to back away. He would take what she allowed him. He would have what he could without hurting her. To take it with him when he left.

Her breasts were a miracle of art, a perfect fit for his seeking hands. He stroked her nipples and his own body grew harder yet as they turned to pebbles under his finger. He pressed his lips against each in turn before deepening the acquaintance. Common sense and intention disappeared into the night as easily as the dying sparks of the fireworks hours before.

The fireworks between them were just beginning.

He drew on an erect nipple and pleasure burst behind his eyelids. He wasn't sure when his right hand sneaked down her flat belly and under the elastic of her bikini bottom. He could only think of the silky feel of her down there.

When and how had the scrap of fabric disappeared?

He could not recall how he ended up between

her parted thighs. Did he part them? He must have. He was drowning in the feel of his hard body pressed against her soft core. He drank in the taste of her mouth, ran a free hand down her side and cupped her buttock—he was supporting himself with the other hand.

And then, only then, did he notice that her body was no longer yielding, that she was holding herself stiff, although not protesting. He pulled away, saw the truth in her eyes even in the dark, and fell to the side, away from her with a soft oath.

"I'm sorry," he said then. "I'm so sorry." And felt like the bastard he was.

"No." She turned to him, her voice shaky. "I don't want you to stop."

He looked at her, bewildered by the soft plea in her eyes that looked black in the night. A couple of seconds passed before the haze in his brain cleared. Then he finally understood what was going on, and it didn't make him feel even a little better.

How could he have not noticed the point where she had stopped wanting it, him, truly wanting, and switched over to going along to prove something, perhaps to herself, perhaps to him?

"I need to—" She couldn't finish the sentence.

What? To complete what they'd started to feel

like any other woman? To make her forget the past? To paint over old, loathsome memories?

He wanted more than anything to help her. "Not like this," he said.

She looked confused and miserable. "I thought you wanted to—"

"Believe me, I do." He gave a strangled laugh. His desire could not be more obvious. It hurt just to think about walking away.

"Just not with me." She looked away.

He reached out and lifted her chin so she could look into his eyes when he spoke. "Only with you. When you're ready."

"I'm ready." Her frustration came through her voice. She pressed against him.

He didn't pull away but took her hand and one by one unfolded the fingers that had been clenched into a tight fist. "This isn't what ready looks like, Sam." He drew a deep breath. "You don't have to rush it."

He pulled her to him and held her, held her tight, felt the way as their hearts thump-thumped against each other. He kissed her hair over and over again, but his lips never once strayed below her forehead. And after a while he felt her relax against him, and her arms came around his back.

He could have happily spent the rest of his life just like that.

The thought slapped him sane with the force of

a tidal wave. Is that what she thought was at the end of this road? Some kind of happy ending? He wasn't that kind of man. He'd never been able to do it in the past. It was only fair to warn her.

But not now. Tomorrow would be soon enough to confront reality. For now, in this moment, she seemed happy and content, and he wanted to give her that if even for a night.

He rose and lifted her into his arms, carried her to the guesthouse, shielding her body with his own from view of the mansion once they were out of the shadows of the palm trees.

Chapter Eight

"Has he been caught?" Tsernyakov asked, a last test for the man about whose fate he was still undecided.

"Not yet," Cavanaugh responded with the truth. "But it's only a matter of time. It's a small island."

Tsernyakov already knew about the hustler from another source. He had wanted to know whether Cavanaugh would try to cover up his own incompetence. The fate of the hustler would not matter long anyhow. "You still have that property in Belize?"

"For now. I'm considering selling it. A large lot is coming up for sale on Little Cayman and I might need the extra capital. Why? You know anything about Belize?" The interest was clear in his voice. Cavanaugh was always game for a good bit of business.

"I know something about the Caymans."

"You think property prices will go down?" He sounded pained by the very idea.

"Next year this time, you can buy that lot for a dime on the dollar. In the meantime, go to Belize."

"It's impossible. Everything I have is invested here."

Tsernyakov scratched his chin. He knew the feeling. He had investments all over the world that he was backpedaling out of, trying his best not to become suspicious.

"I suggest you free up as much capital as you can and go to Belize."

Dead silence ruled on the other end. Then, "That serious? Are you sure?"

"I wouldn't, of course, presume to make decisions for my friends," he responded cordially.

"Okay, okay. By when? I have time, right? How many months? A year?"

"Two weeks," he said.

His own ranch high up in the Andes Mountains was already prepared. He owned a thousand acres in the most isolated spot imaginable, including two villages and a small copper mine. His most trusted men were fortifying the place even now and laying in supplies.

The virus he was nearly ready to hand over to his buyers would wreak enough havoc to bring about a new world order. Not that he wasn't happy with his life in the current one. He had achieved as much as any man could under the given circumstances. But what if all the rules and laws were thrown out and life returned to the survival of the fittest? What could he achieve then?

He wasn't greedy. He regularly gave to the poor. He had donated a small fortune to the hospital that treated his mother. He supported education through seven different grants, although he himself had never had formal training. Simple truth was, he was a megalomaniac. He embraced that and the boundless motivation and energy it brought to his life. Why not have him at the top? As much misery as there was in this world, who said he couldn't do better?

Yes, it would all start with unspeakable tragedy, but in truth, he was doing a service to humankind.

CAVANAUGH STARED at the memo in front of him, something he had brought home from work the week before. He didn't even see the printed words on the paper. All he could see was the deadline Tsernyakov had given him. He looked up the date. Two weeks from now. November 27. He had circled the date in red ink over and over again.

Sweat beaded on his forehead. How on earth was he going to accomplish all he had to do in two weeks? He felt ill at the thought of how much he was going to lose. How long had Tsernyakov known this? And what was it, exactly, that he knew?

What could damage an area as big as the islands?

A dirty bomb?

But why now and why here?

He dabbed his forehead, wadded up the paper then squashed it between his hands.

What about his life here? If what Tsernyakov was warning him about did turn out to be a dirty bomb, it could be years before he could safely come back.

Damn, damn the man for not saying more. And yet, he couldn't sustain any kind of anger. Behind that, and the panic of it all, a much stronger feeling ruled his emotions—relief that Tsernyakov chose to warn him at all.

He thought of his guests, sleeping in the guest-house. He had to send them home. Without arousing suspicion. But as he pondered them, he changed his mind. He liked this estate and he liked to entertain. Who knew when he was going to get another chance? He was due a little fun before he had to give up the life he had worked so hard to build.

Let them stay. He had a lot of work to do, but he needed distraction in between, too. And his guests provided that, especially delectable little Sam.

She was impressed by him, he could tell. He liked feeling flattered. He could almost feel her lithe body under him as she finally surrendered to him. She was skittish. He didn't mind that. Taming her would feel that much sweeter. It would be his last indulgence before he left for Belize. And who knew, if she behaved herself, he might even take her with him.

No matter what her boyfriend thought about it.

David Moretti had surprised him. He was much stronger than he'd thought at his first impression of the man. And David didn't like Philippe around Sam, not a bit. Too bad. Because Philippe was used to getting what he wanted. One way or the other.

He pulled a sheet of clean paper from the printer and began writing names in a long row. They weren't people he would, in turn, save. There'd be none of those. He couldn't afford a leak. Tsernyakov would never forgive a betrayed confidence. It was a list of those he needed to make his exit from life as he knew it as quick and smooth as possible.

SAM LAY IN BED and stared at the ceiling, listening to Reese's even breathing next to her. She hadn't been able to sleep since they had come in for the night. He didn't seem to have that problem.

He had placed her on her side of the bed, gently, kissed her then went for a shower. When he'd finally come to bed, he'd turned his back to her and wished her a sleepy-sounding good-night, which she took for a fake until she realized after five minutes or so that he was truly sleeping.

For the last couple of days they'd barely left each other's sight, had been in almost constant physical contact, at first to get used to it so their charade would be believable and now because the big performance was on. It had gotten to the point that she was beginning to miss him when they weren't touching.

And after what had happened on the beach…

She actually wasn't sure what had happened or why it had stopped. Maybe he remembered who she was and where she'd come from. Or had she misread him?

She stared at his wide, naked back in the semi-darkness of the bedroom. Extended her hand. Pulled it back just before they would have touched. She wanted to feel the warmth of his skin under her palms, the smooth hills and valleys of muscles, be enveloped in the strength that radiated from him. If she snuggled up to him—pretending to have rolled over in her sleep—would he wake?

Bad idea. She forced her eyes closed. He had made it clear that the touchy-feely part of the night was over.

Kissing and touching a man could feel pretty damn good. That was a revelation to her. Physical contact didn't have to hurt. She'd known that on a theoretical level. She had attended high school— sporadically and for brief snippets of time. She had gone to public libraries, mostly for the bathrooms, but she had read, too. She had snuck into movie theaters and seen the chick flicks. She understood that some people thought they fell in love and had sex for the fun of it. It hadn't truly connected with her, however, until now.

Reese Moretti had been the only man who had ever taken her clothes off without her putting up a fight, who had ever moved on top of her without her trying her best to break his nose. She had been thrilled by that. She could control the brief flashes of panic. She hadn't fought, she hadn't run. She could have done it with him, probably, all the way. Would that have made her normal? She had wanted that, wanted it still. But he had called it quits.

What was wrong with her?

And what was she going to do when this morning, as soon as the sun came up, it would be back to business as usual, the two of them playing the role of lovers for Cavanaugh's sake? After last night, how on earth was she going to handle it?

Voices filtered through the open window. She sat up, careful not to wake Reese, then slipped from the bed and went to look. Not much seemed to be happening. The voices came from the direction of Cavanaugh's mansion. She couldn't see much through the palm trees that stood by the guesthouse.

She glanced at the door. She could pretend to go for a late-night swim. Except, Philippe knew she was a bad swimmer. He wouldn't buy that.

She leaned over the end of the balcony, praying for some wind to ruffle the palm fronds so that she might catch a glimpse. Whatever was going on, whoever was there, they'd be gone before that happened.

She blew the hair out of her face, frustrated, glancing up at the roof. If she were a few feet higher, she could see over the trees.

For a split second, she thought about waking Reese, but then changed her mind. It didn't seem necessary. She'd go up on the roof, take a look around, come down. She glanced at her dark gray cotton shorts and tank top. Shouldn't have any trouble with blending into the shadows.

She stepped up to the edge of the railing then reached for the roof, swung her legs up. Oops. She nearly kicked off a roof tile. She stilled when she gained purchase. Okay. Other leg. Pull. She lay on the edge of the roof, waited again for any sound that she'd been discovered. When she was fairly certain that nobody had been awakened by the slight noise she had made, she got up into a crouch and climbed higher.

She could still hear the voices and now see the front door of Philippe's mansion, but nobody was there. Where had they gone? Maybe they were coming down the path around to the front of the guesthouse. If she went over the peak, she should be able to see them.

Too late again. The voices now came from under the overhang. She had to scoot all the way to the edge, extra careful this time. If a tile rattled under her, they would hear.

She moved foothold by foothold. A slight noise drew her attention from the other side of the roof, which she could no longer see. She froze. What was that? She waited. It had to be a bird. A seagull. Who else would be crazy enough to be out on the roof at three in the morning? She had to move or whoever she was trying to catch a glimpse of would go inside.

She inched closer, on her stomach now, as low as possible so the moonlight wouldn't cast her shadow on the ground below. The man and woman were whispering, but she could make out a few words.

"You know how it is," the woman said.

"I thought— I was really hoping this time. I love you. Can't that be enough?"

"We are not the same kind of people. I would disappoint you."

"Never." The word was spoken with heated passion.

"I love money."

"I would show you how unimportant it is when you have true love."

There was a moment of pause, then, "I wish I could believe that."

Sam leaned over. She could only see the guy, a member of Cavanaugh's security, Jack somebody. The woman was standing in the doorway. And because she was whispering, Sam couldn't recognize her voice, either.

"You mean nothing to Philippe," the man said.

"He's my biggest client. That's enough."

The man moved forward and Sam was pretty sure some heated kissing was going on below.

"When you change your mind, I'll be here," the guy said then strode away.

She flattened herself to the roof and waited until the man passed out of sight, not daring to get up in case he turned back one last time. Once she was sure he couldn't see her, she scampered up to the spine of the roof then over it, down on the other side.

For a second she thought she saw a shadow on the balcony that wasn't her own, but it must have been a trick of her eyes. She lowered herself, snuck back into the room. Reese was sleeping in the same position she had left him. She snuck out the suite's front door and crept to the top of the stairs. The guesthouse had three more suites, with a couple in each.

Had the woman already gone inside while Sam was coming down from the roof? Frustration tightened her fingers over the railing. Then she caught a glimpse of movement below.

Eva meandered down the hall with an armful of folders. She stopped, leaned against the wall, looking stressed and nervous. She stayed there for a full minute before taking a deep breath and opening the door to the suite she shared with Derrick then going inside.

She'd come from the mansion. Sam was sure of that. And she was also sure she wasn't there for a quickie with one of the security guards. She'd had business folders. Most likely, Philippe had called her for a meeting, then the lovesick guard had escorted her back to the guesthouse to plead his case.

The question was, what was so important to Philippe that he needed to discuss it with Eva in the middle of the night? Was she stressed out by that or by the security guard's words?

Up until now, she hadn't acted like a woman who would be distressed because a man wanted something from her. On the contrary.

But if her upset was due to Philippe— Sam stepped back from the railing. She would have given anything to find out what their meeting was about. Was the woman simply Philippe's real-estate agent or was she more, an accomplice perhaps? Was she part of his shady businesses? Was she another link to Tsernyakov?

They had to find a way to figure out what had happened at the Cavanaugh mansion tonight.

SAM AND REESE WERE GOING for their morning run on the beach when they saw Eva and her boy-friend—a term that could be only loosely used as both had switched partners freely during the week—packing up their car. The boyfriend went inside for the rest of their luggage.

"I'd better go talk to her," Reese said and left Sam to continue on her own. The strained silence between them had been driving him crazy, anyway.

He'd been up all night, an arm's length from her as she tossed and turned, missing her body snuggled against his. He'd gotten used to her sleeping in his arms each night, even if he had carefully pulled away each morning before she woke. She hadn't had any nightmares since that first time. Neither had he.

But tossing and turning and walking around wasn't all she'd done the night before. He'd followed her onto the roof, making sure he was there if she needed him, making sure she got back down okay. She was sexy as hell, crawling in a crouch like a superspy in nothing but some skimpy sleepwear. If frustration could kill a man, he would be joyriding a hearse right now. What in the hell was wrong with him?

She was a contrast of vulnerability and strength, simmering hot beauty and innocence. Combinations that drove him crazy.

Why couldn't he put her out of his head like he had been able to do with all the others since Natalie?

Because she isn't like all the others.

Good luck trying to maintain professional distance when she was sleeping in his bed every night. The sooner the mission was over, the better. The temptation was getting too difficult to resist. He would see she got out safely then hop on the first plane back to Africa.

He kept his attention on Eva, who was leaning against the car, looking sullen. Sam had told him about seeing her leaving Cavanaugh's place a little after 3:00 a.m. with a stack of folders, looking distraught. Chances were, Eva would be more likely to talk to him than to Sam, for whom she seemed to hold a politely veiled dislike.

If that didn't work, their backup plan had been to break into her room when everyone was at the beach. Which seemed unlikely now since she appeared to be leaving.

"Morning. Need any help?" He put on the best, most charming smile he could eke out. David was the resident charmer in the family. Reese had no patience for putting up a charade and playing down the list of all those courtship rituals. Either someone liked him for who he was or they didn't. According to David, he was a little rough around the edges. The assessment didn't bother him a bit.

"You're so nice to offer." Eva's smile didn't reach her eyes.

"You're not leaving early, are you?" He lifted a suitcase into the trunk.

"Business calls." Now she looked decidedly annoyed.

He put a look of regret on his face. "Don't you get to take a little vacation? Turn the phone off."

"Wish I could." She ran her fingers over her hair, assuring everything was in order. "But this cranky client, I need to keep. Can't afford to tick off someone who brings in eighty percent of my business."

"Right. We all have those." He nodded. "So some big real-estate coup is going on? Are prices about to skyrocket? Should I buy a little something quick so I can be in on it?"

She shrugged and rolled her eyes. "Nothing's

going on. The man is just insane. One day it's *buy everything you can get your hands on,* the next it's, *sell everything you can get rid of in a hurry, must complete all transactions ASAP.* Like I'm some miracle worker and can offload millions of dollars' worth of property in a matter of days." She caught herself. "Sorry. Didn't get much sleep last night. I'm a little on the cranky side."

"Last one," the boyfriend, Derrick, called as he came out the door with a suitcase large enough for a person to fit inside.

How much clothing did Eva need for a week-long beach party? Sam had only brought a gym bag. He liked that about her, that she was a down-to-earth, no-nonsense, no-frills type of woman.

"Well, we're off. Have fun." Derrick nodded to him.

"Good to meet you both." Reese shook their hands. "If I make up my mind about that vacation home near the beach, I'll give you a call," he told Eva. She'd been trying to talk him into one the day before.

"Please do." She got into the open-top convertible. "You have my card. I'm about to list a dozen more properties. You could probably get a decent price since the seller is in a hurry."

Derrick pulled away from the house and up to the gate.

Reese watched them leave before he turned and jogged back to Sam, unable to stop reflecting on the differences between the two women. Then he got angry at himself for doing nothing but thinking of Sam all morning. What was wrong with him? He was here to do a job.

He needed to keep that first and foremost in his mind.

"SO WE PRETEND that we had a fight and I'm going to cozy up to Cavanaugh out of spite." Sam summed up her plan.

Reese put down his fork. He had inhaled his eggs in seconds. "I don't like the idea. You agreed that whatever had to be done we'll do together."

She tried to be patient. "We can't seduce Cavanaugh together."

"You're not seducing him." His nostrils actually flared as he said that.

Well, duh. Not all the way. "What other choice do we have? We need information." The call list on Cavanaugh's phone had been informational, but didn't net them an immediate connection to Tsernyakov. The last phone number they tracked belonged to a fictional businessman who worked for a fictional business at a fictional address in the backwoods of the Republic of Georgia. No other calls had been made before or since. Was

Tsernyakov so paranoid that he used a new cell phone for every call he made? He could certainly afford it.

"What we know is that Cavanaugh likely got a call from someone who might be connected to Tsernyakov, or the man himself, the day before yesterday. Then last night, in the middle of the night, he decides to sell a bunch of property he owns on the islands. Why?"

. "He got some interesting piece of news."

"Why wait a day to act on it?"

"Maybe he wanted to get confirmation, or maybe he got another call." Reese shrugged.

"Eva said he was obsessed with buying up property on Little Cayman. Now all of a sudden he's selling it? Whatever he found out has to be big."

"We don't know for sure that he is the client Eva talked about."

"Ninety-nine percent sure. She was with him till dawn, leaving with a stack of folders. Why would Philippe want to sell?"

"There could be a fantastic new investment opportunity somewhere else and he might need the money in a hurry, although that is not likely."

"Why?" Seemed plausible to her.

"He has enough collateral. He could borrow from a bank or from one of his shady friends. Why sell prime property he had painstakingly collected over the years? And selling in a hurry won't be to his advantage. He's unlikely to get top price."

"Then what? Is he afraid something bad will happen?"

"That would be my guess. He found out that his investment might lose value."

"Soon," she added. "He is in a hurry."

"We need to know what is going down and when. Okay?"

"Okay."

He held her gaze. "We'll have a fight."

Chapter Nine

Tsernyakov's body hummed with adrenaline as he walked through the doors of his suite. He'd been in the business for so long he had thought he'd seen just about everything. But this current deal topped it all. He was about to change the course of history. He loved the heady rush that came with the thought.

He set the box he'd been carrying by the door and kicked off his Italian-leather loafers, tossed his silk tie on the back of the Louis XIV chair in the foyer, his suit jacket on top of it.

Alexandra came from her room, wearing the cream-colored silk pajamas he had picked out for her on their last trip to Marks & Spencer. "It's you." Her face brightened at the sight of him.

"Can't sleep?" It was two in the morning. "Are you well?"

She took a deep breath and pushed her hair behind her ears. "Fine. Just restless."

So was he. He smiled. "I have a present for you."

Her full lips stretched even wider as she came to him. "You don't have to give me presents all the time."

"I like seeing you smile." He took her hand and led her to the box. "Go on, open it."

Her squeal of delight told him that his present hit the mark.

"She is beautiful." Alexandra was hugging the furry white puppy with the pink bow around her neck. "What kind is it?"

"Kuvasz. A rare Hungarian breed. They are endlessly loyal and fiercely protective."

"She's perfect. Thank you, thank you, thank you." She pressed her lips to his cheeks.

And he decided that was no longer enough.

"I need to wind down. Want to watch a movie together and play with the puppy for a while?" He headed for his wing of the spacious apartment and she followed.

She sat on the floor with the puppy and he sat next to her. He'd been trying hard to keep up a youthful appearance. And it wasn't all appearance. He was in good shape, had always taken care of himself. The two plastic surgeries designed to alter his face enough so video profiling at airports couldn't identify him also took off a couple of years. And being with Alexandra made him *feel* younger.

He played along, watching her, laughing with her until the puppy finally knocked herself out and curled up to sleep in the middle of the antique Chinese rug.

He leaned closer to Alexandra and drew a hand down her silk-covered arm. "You grow more beautiful every single day."

Her shy smile brought out a response in him. He'd been sitting there, mere centimeters away from her all night, watching the way her top hung on her pert breasts, the way the pants hugged her buttocks. She wore nothing under her pajamas. He was primed and ready.

"I have to confess something." He looked away. "But I'm worried that it might ruin our friendship."

"Nothing could ruin our friendship." This time it was she who took his hand.

"The last few weeks, months, since you came into my life—I cannot tell you how much happiness you brought to me. I realize you probably can't ever look at me as anything else but— I should never have told you this." He held her hand. "I think I might be falling in love with you. There, now I scared you. I'm sorry." He looked away.

"No. No. I just—" She sounded genuinely surprised.

He took advantage of that and leaned in for a kiss.

She didn't push him away immediately. And then he made sure she wouldn't. Her body was restless, her mind sleepy—the perfect combination. His hand came up and cupped her breast, and he was gratified to feel her nipple harden against his palm.

She had a healthy twenty-year-old body that responded well to skillful stimulation. And he had plenty of experience. Slowly, so that she was probably not even aware of what was happening, he pushed her down to the carpet. Tonight, he would get what he wanted.

"ONE OF PHILIPPE'S MEN IS TAKING everyone out for an afternoon of deep-sea fishing." Reese was coming through the door.

Sam yanked the ruffled top over her head. She'd just changed out of her bikini to go to lunch at the main house. She caught a flare of heat in Reese's gaze as he turned his back to her. Her pulse quickened. She kept her eyes on his wide shoulders as she pulled her shorts right over the bikini bottom.

"Sounds like fun, right? I'm done."

He turned around, looked her over. "You look nice."

How stupid that the small comment would fluster her. "Thanks." She busied herself straightening up the room.

"The question is why."

"Why what?" She looked at him.

"Why does Cavanaugh want everyone out of the way?"

"He has some business to take care of?"

He nodded slowly.

She considered that. "Maybe someone he doesn't want us to see is coming here. Why would he have a party with a ton of guests if he is expecting some secret partner in crime?"

"Maybe it's unexpected business."

"I think lunch is going to make me sick to my stomach. I can't go out on the boat like that," she said.

He gave her an approving grin. "The attentive kind of guy that I am, naturally, I'll stay to take care of my woman."

Her heart gave a little thud at the "my woman" part.

THE TROUBLE WITH faking sickness was that she couldn't be out there frolicking in the surf, keeping an eye on who was coming to see Cavanaugh. Neither could Reese, who was supposed to be holding her hand and all that. And they didn't have a direct line of vision either to the front gate of the estate or to the front door of the mansion from any of the windows in their suite.

Reese watched Sam pace the living room. She

was a bundle of nervous energy. "I think it's time we brought out the secret weapon," he said.

She stopped and stared at him. "How do we know where they'll be meeting?"

"My bet would be Cavanaugh's living room."

"And if they used his office?"

He shook his head. "From what you said, it looked like his private lair. Had only one chair, his."

She nodded, but still looked doubtful.

He understood. "There is no guarantee where the meeting will be, if there is a meeting. Could be he just wants a quiet day for himself."

She took a slow breath. "But most likely, there is something going on. And if there is, it will be here somewhere. If he was going to an off-site meeting, he wouldn't need to send everyone off fishing."

He nodded.

"And if there is a meeting and it's here, the most likely place is the living room. We have to prepare for the best possible scenario and have a backup plan in case plan A doesn't pan out."

He grinned at her. She was beginning to talk like Law and Tarasov. Obviously, she'd paid attention during her training. He had a feeling Sam paid attention to a lot of things. She was sharp and capable, quick on the uptake and not easily intimidated. He was as comfortable working with her as with his team, which was saying something.

"So I go over to ask for some antinausea medicine for you. When nobody's looking, I'll spray something in the living room with the micro-transmitters. Then we hope for the best."

"Are the odds always this long? In your work," she asked.

"Pretty much. My mother tells me I gave her every single gray hair she has."

"I bet." She was smiling, shaking her head. "You seem like the wilder of the two."

He took that as a compliment. "Wildest of the bunch. I have three sisters."

She seemed surprised.

"Everyone is married, except me. Eleven nieces and nephews." He wasn't sure why he was telling her that. He normally didn't share any of his private life with the people he protected.

"So what's it like to have a big family?" Her tone had a wishful tinge to it.

"Crazy." He grinned. "Wonder why I spend most of my time out of the country?" But then he grew serious as he thought about them. "I love my family. They're the most important thing to me in the world."

"More important than your job?"

"No contest."

"Are you close?"

"Very. Most of us live in or around Boston."

"That must be weird," she mused.

"We like to think of it as normal."

"Didn't mean it in a bad way," she said quickly. "To me, normal just seems weird. You know what I mean?"

He nodded because he did, and wished it could have been normal for her in the past. His family would swallow her up, in a good way. Not that they would ever meet. And even if they did, could Sam handle the boisterous Moretti bunch?

"So what's it like to have someone worry about you? Does it stop you from doing stuff?"

"Hardly."

"Nobody ever worried about me," she said pensively, then shrugged as if it didn't matter. Then a moment later she was smiling and rolling her eyes. "God, that sounds like I'm wallowing in self-pity. I'm not. Really. There are plenty of people out there who have it a lot rougher than I did."

"You're not wallowing," he assured her. And even if she were, she would be entitled to it. "And I do worry about you." He pointed to his temple. "See this gray hair? I got it since we've been working together."

She held his gaze for an endless minute, a range of emotions flitting across her face. Then she shut them off and put them all away, turning toward the window.

"You'd better get over to the estate before whomever Philippe is expecting gets here. They might not let you in later," she said.

"YOU WANT ME to take over the hatchery?" the visitor was asking.

Sam pressed a finger to the chickpea-size receiver in her ear. Reese had a matching one. The inconspicuous little gadget could be ground into dust under the heel of a shoe in a fraction of a second if there was any danger of it being discovered. The matching set came with Ferrarella's "secret weapon."

"Philippe has a turtle hatchery on the tip of the island," she explained to Reese.

He nodded.

"Other opportunities opened up to me someplace else. I'm simplifying. Returning to core business," Philippe said.

What? Sam listened, impatient for specific details. Was there some new big deal with Tsernyakov in the works?

"Why me?" The visitor sounded suspicious.

"You know the full potential of the place."

Reese looked at her. "You know what that means. He is running something illegal here that this guy could continue. And if our mystery man took over, he wouldn't have to worry about shutting that off and covering his tracks there."

She was pretty sure he was right. "But why is he pulling out?"

Reese shook his head. "I have a feeling it would be instrumental for our mission to get the answer to that."

"I have some capital that will be freed up after the end of the year," the visitor was saying.

"I need to move sooner than that."

Names. Come on. Say his name, Sam willed the man. They needed an identity, even if assumed, Brant could investigate.

"Why? What's wrong with the hatchery?" The guy sounded suspicious.

"Hatchery is fine. There is a business opportunity I want to take advantage of. It has a deadline."

"I need to take a look at the operation. Have to check some figures."

"Of course."

"You can hold it for two weeks?"

"Until the end of this week," Philippe said, "I won't mention it to anyone else."

"Give me one full week at least."

There was a moment of silence. "All right, a full week. But the full purchase price is due on the day of signing the sale agreement."

"If I decide to buy, I'll get the money."

Glasses clinked together.

"You did this place up nice," the visitor said after a while. "Business been good?"

"Can't complain," Cavanaugh said, but there was an odd tinge to his voice.

"I don't suppose you'll tell me what this new business is that you're getting into?"

Cavanaugh laughed. "Not a chance."

"I thought we were friends," the guy said with mock hurt.

"Not that good of friends."

"You know what I like about you? You never change. Greedy bastard to the end."

Cavanaugh laughed again. "You've made some money off me over the years."

"That I have."

"Now you'll make some more."

Glasses clinked again.

"So," the guy said after a while. "Where are your throngs of beautiful women? They all figured out the ugliness behind your smarmy charm?"

Cavanaugh tsked. "That's just green-eyed jealousy talking. They're out with the boat."

"You were afraid they'd see me and begin wondering what they were doing with some old French goat?"

"Frenchmen are known for love. What are shady Brazilians known for?" Cavanaugh shot back.

Sam and Reese exchanged a look. At least now they knew this much. The guy was Brazilian.

"How is the new wife, anyway?" Philippe asked.

"Not any better than the first three," the visitor responded. "I'm an eternal optimist. Maybe I'll luck out with the next."

"Cheaper to keep lovers."

"I want heirs, not bastards."

"Suit yourself," Cavanaugh said. "Just remember, heirs have a tendency to become impatient for their inheritance."

"Sentimental old fool, isn't he?" Reese said in a voice thick with irony.

"They are done talking business," Sam stated the obvious.

"He'll be leaving soon."

The conversation hadn't netted nearly as much information as they had hoped for.

"We need a picture of the guy," she said.

They waited until the men were saying goodbye and made getting-up kind of noises. Sam used the time to wash all vestiges of makeup from her face, making herself look as pale as possible. When she was done, she messed up her hair.

They walked downstairs together. She put a

drained expression on her face and looped an arm around Reese's neck. He supported her with an arm around her back as they stepped out the door.

She made sure the finger that had the camera ring on pointed toward the Cavanaugh mansion at all times as they began a slow trek toward the water's edge, making sure to leave a clean line of vision between them and the mansion.

First, the security guys appeared.

"Look toward the water," Reese said into her ear.

She did so, making sure the camera was pointed toward the house still. She worked the tiny button with her thumb, taking pictures blindly.

She risked a glance from the corner of her eye. A guy she hadn't seen before was getting into a car with tinted windows. Roberto was making a beeline for them. She managed to take another picture, hoping she had aimed right. Then she made a point of closing her eyes and resting her head on Reese's shoulder.

"Are you okay?" Roberto asked when he was close enough.

She looked at him. "Thought some fresh air might do me good."

He stood in a way to block the car from her view, but she could hear the engine start up.

"How bad is it?" He sounded genuinely concerned. "Want me to take you to the hospital?"

"I'll take her if she's not better in a couple of hours. Thanks," Reese said.

Roberto hesitated, giving him a hostile look. "Take it easy," he told Sam before strolling away.

The black sedan that had carried the visitor was nowhere to be seen.

HE MISSED HER. They'd had their "fight" as soon as she "recovered." She'd barely set foot in their suite since. Reese watched from afar as Sam flirted with Cavanaugh. She was lightening up after having relayed to him their terrible row that had supposedly taken place behind the closed doors of their suite. Cavanaugh had consoled her, naturally. She was now playing the part that it had worked and she was over Reese already. Reese clamped his jaw shut as he watched them. If Cavanaugh put his hands on her one more time— He looked away, disgusted with himself. What? What was he going to do? Nothing. She was doing her job.

Still, he didn't have to like it.

He hit another golf ball on the sand. He'd been doing that with more and more force, he realized. How had everything gotten here? Complicated. Not that his job was normally simple, but his main objectives used to be more straightforward. *Protect the client.* Or, if he'd been called in after something bad had happened, *retrieve the client.*

He never got emotionally involved, not to this level.

Had he lost his edge? If so, he would do everyone a favor if he retired from the business.

There. Two months ago that thought would have been unimaginable. Right now he could actually picture spending some time Stateside. With Sam. That last bit was the most frightening part of all.

He wasn't what she needed.

Damn. He hit another ball. What did he know about what she needed?

What did he want?

No. He didn't dare ask that question.

His cell phone rang. Brant Law. He took the call.

"What's up?"

"We took another look at the turtle hatchery and got some new information. Looks like a good portion of his workforce there is illegal. He ships illegal immigrants in from South America, they stop on Grand Cayman and work free for him in payment for the trip, then eventually he moves them on and smuggles them into the U.S. When they get there, most of them are forced to enter some sort of prostitution ring that also has something to do with him."

"He's a prince among men. Thanks," Reese said before he hung up.

Cavanaugh was caressing Sam's face.

Reese gritted his teeth. The way the guy was touching her bothered him more than the illegal drugs, the human trafficking and his link with Tsernyakov put together. The business with Sam was personal. He could cheerfully have strangled the man.

What were they talking about now? Sam looked amused. She hadn't looked amused that night when Reese had touched her. At first she'd felt the connection between them, too, he was sure. Then at one point something had shifted. And although she hadn't protested, she was as scared as the proverbial sacrificial virgin. And yet she was willing to go through with it. But that wasn't what he wanted. He wanted her to feel what he felt.

Oh, hell. Now he was admitting to feelings?

He kicked the sand.

Damn.

He was falling for her, wasn't he?

His turn to be scared. Especially when he looked her way again and just caught the last glimpse as Cavanaugh escorted her inside his lair.

"Coming for a ride with us?" A couple of the other guests were going out on WaveRunners.

He shook his head. "Later."

He moved closer to the house and took inventory of the security guys in sight. Four of them lounged in the shade at various locations.

How many were inside?

What was Cavanaugh doing with Sam in there?

He pushed the unwanted pictures out of his mind. He couldn't focus on that. No sense in losing his cool. He couldn't help her that way.

He was doing his part of the job and she was doing hers. She was tough. She had handled a lot in her life already. She could handle this. He kept repeating that in his head. It didn't make him feel any better.

He managed to hold out for a whole hour before he called her on her cell.

"Everything okay?"

"Don't call me," she said, then moved the phone away from her mouth and talked to Cavanaugh. "It's David. He wants to make up." Then came back to him. "I'm going to hang out here for tonight. Philippe gave me one of the guest rooms in the main house. You can stay or go. I really don't care." With that she hung up.

He drew a deep breath. She brought out his protective instincts in spades, and no wonder, considering her past and his. He was terrified of letting down another woman he should have been protecting. But with Sam, the situation was different. At the moment, facing danger was her job. And it wasn't altogether bad for her, although he hated to admit that.

Every new success brought self-confidence and a sense of strength, knowing that she could handle other difficult situations in the future. He had worked with plenty of people who'd had bad experiences, had been traumatized in the past. He knew the way to getting over the fear wasn't to stay in a cocoon. He wanted her to have a full life.

She'd gone a long way toward achieving that since he'd met her. A lot of the skittishness had left her, the prickliness that had surfaced at the beginning as a means of defense.

He'd been a parachuting instructor. Doing tandem jumps with his students had been fine— being there, knowing he was in control, that he could protect them. But eventually he'd had to let them go, had to trust them to jump on their own so they could truly soar.

He wanted that for Sam. She was smart and tough. She knew how to get the job done. He was going to let her. Which didn't mean he wouldn't be standing by and watching her back.

He was close enough to the mansion to see the upstairs guest bedroom through which she had gone in before. Was that her room now? He looked at the security camera on the covered porch below it and aimed the next golf ball. It hit its target, moving the camera to the left an inch or so. That should be enough. Just in case he needed to get up there in a hurry.

And he did, not an hour later.

"Philippe is going out. I'm not sure how long he'll be gone," Sam said over the phone. "I need help opening the safe."

He was down by the beach by then, but made his way back to the mansion, lay down in a hammock for a minute until he made sure none of Cavanaugh's men were around. Then he sauntered over to the patio. The security camera's angle was hopefully off enough not to give him away. He climbed the column and heaved himself over the edge of the balcony railing, kept low as he made his way to the door.

The room was empty, but Sam's flip-flops stood next to the bed, a sign letting him know he was in the right place. He opened the door slowly and identified each door in the hallway: gym, cleaning closet, Cavanaugh's office. Sam had given him descriptions after she'd been up here the first time.

When he got level with the office, he realized the door was open to a nearly imperceptible crack. He paused, heard movement inside.

"Sam?" he whispered.

If it was someone else in there, he would claim he'd come to beg her to come back to him. But he doubted anyone would be allowed in Cavanaugh's office in his absence.

The door opened and Sam reached out to pull him in.

"Are you okay?"

"Fine." She sounded impatient as she closed the door.

"What are you doing here? I thought the safe was in the bedroom." He glanced around. The laser beams she'd told him about were nowhere to be seen.

He wanted to grab her and just hold her for a second.

She was already moving away from him. "That one doesn't have anything in it except his passports and some cash. And some diadem from Marie Antoinette he just got at an auction." She rolled her eyes. "He wants to make sure I know he's the richest guy on the block."

"How did you get in here?"

She led him behind Cavanaugh's desk where a Caribbean landscape in oil had been pushed away from the wall, revealing a steel plate embedded in concrete. "The bedroom has a security system, too. I saw the code when he punched it in. I took a chance."

"I don't suppose the safe uses the same code?" He ran his fingers over the keypad.

She shook her head. "I already tried." She was looking at him expectantly.

He hated to disappoint her. "I don't know anything about safes except how to blow one up." And they had no access to explosives, nor could they afford to use any even if they had. Along with the safe, they would also blow their cover.

He took a picture of the safe with his cell phone and sent it to Brant Law along with a request for information on what they could possibly do with the steel trap. If they were lucky, the information would come in before Cavanaugh got back. If not, they would have to try again later.

"Have you searched the office?" he asked Sam as he turned his attention to Cavanaugh's desk.

"Roughly. I haven't been in here that long. I was focused on the safe."

He riffled through the papers on the edge of the desk. Bills for the house and the grounds, security, power, water. The desk drawers were locked. He grabbed the silver letter opener and went to work with that.

Sam was digging through the paper basket. "I saw this in the movies," she said.

The first drawer popped open. He dug through

the stack of papers—shrunk-down copies of blue-prints and old contracts. Nothing he could make anything out of. He tried the second drawer.

She put a handful of wadded-up yellow sticky notes on the table and began to unfold them.

The sound of knocking came from outside.

They both went still.

A second passed before he realized whoever it was, wasn't knocking on the office door.

"Ma'am." The voice came from down the hall, followed by more knocking. "Will you come down to the dining room for lunch or would you like your meal to be brought up?"

Sam went to the door.

He could hear another door opening.

"Ma'am?"

She peeked out then stepped outside.

"Looking for me?" he heard after a second. "I went over to check out the gym. I think I'll hang out there until Philippe comes back. Is that okay?"

"Certainly, ma'am," came the response. "Where would you like your lunch?"

"I think I'll wait for Philippe."

"Of course. Just let me know if you change your mind or if you need anything. The kitchen is extension five on the house phone."

"Thanks."

Reese listened for the sound of shoes on the

marble stairs and heard it a moment later. Then, in another second or two, Sam was back.

"Well done." He cupped her face without intending to, then caught himself and let go.

She looked away. "Let's get to work."

He popped the second drawer and flipped through the stack of data-storage CDs. No designation on them, except for a single six-digit number on each. "What are these?"

She glanced over and shook her head, opening one sticky note after another. "What's this?" She held one out for him.

A date, November 27, was written on it in black ink, outlined over and over, circled several times in red.

If they weren't specifically looking for a date, they wouldn't have thought anything of it. But from what Eva had said, it was clear that Cavanaugh had some kind of deadline. Was this it?

"What else?" He turned his attention to the paper basket, as well.

What he got were nearly empty papers, with no useful information. Maybe not for Cavanaugh in any case. Reese flipped open his phone and entered the URL at the bottom of the pages.

"Anything?" Sam looked up from what she was doing.

"Bad news." He took a slow breath, cold

spreading in his stomach. "It seems our friend has gained a recent interest in how to survive nuclear contamination."

Sam went pale.

He wasn't feeling too well, either.

What was Tsernyakov up to? How much did Cavanaugh know?

"Is his laptop still in his bedroom?" he asked.

"I don't know. I went back to my room as he was leaving. Didn't want him to get suspicious that I'm snooping around."

"Let's check it out then." He went to the door and looked out. "All clear."

Sam went first, in case someone did come up the stairs. She was supposed to be here. Reese wasn't. After she reached the bedroom door and looked around, she signaled to him that it was okay to follow.

She punched the security code into the system. "It's okay now."

"Why doesn't it arm as soon as the door is open?" he asked.

She pointed to the corner of the ceiling. "It's set to a motion detector. You don't quite come within its range until you're about two steps into the room."

He closed the door behind them so if someone did come up, their presence here wouldn't be immediately obvious.

The bedroom was spacious, twice as large as the office, with a round bed sprawling by the far wall. Cavanaugh kept quite a collection of art here, abstract nudes for the most part. He zeroed in on the laptop on the nightstand.

Of course, it was password protected.

"We need to get Carly in here," Sam said.

"Would be nice. Or get the laptop out to her." Both options seemed impossible.

"We could take it right now and leave the estate."

He thought about that for a second. "And if there's nothing useful on it about the planned attack? Our covers would be blown, the one chance anyone has to get close to Tsernyakov. We can't risk everything on odds this long."

She paced the room. "Okay. You're right. What if I called Carly? Could she walk us through it?"

A little light began to blink on the bottom of the sign-in screen.

"We'd better hurry," he said. "Looks like the battery is dying."

And it seemed that wasn't their only problem.

There was some noise downstairs—a door slamming, footsteps coming up. Then Cavanaugh's voice on the stairs.

Chapter Ten

"What are you two doing here?" Philippe watched them from the door with cold calculation.

"David won't leave me alone." Sam rushed to him. "I came in here to get away from him and he followed me. He's being a complete bastard about this." She threw a loathing look at Reese while pressing her body to Cavanaugh's. "I know you would never be rude to a guest, but can't you make him understand that he's worn out his welcome?" She was giving an award-worthy performance.

Reese watched Cavanaugh. His features didn't soften. His right hand was fisted. The cold feeling in Reese's stomach said *this was it*. The jig was up. But it wasn't in him to give up without trying to salvage the situation.

"You shut your mouth," he yelled at Sam like a man at the end of his rope. "You came with me, you'll leave with me. That's the way it's done. I love you." His heart skipped a beat as he said those words. "What do you think he wants from you?" He glared accusingly at Cavanaugh. "How long do you think he'll play with you before he casts you aside?"

"Don't you tell me to shut up!" Sam grabbed a cast-iron candleholder from the shelf next to her and hurled it at him.

He caught it handily. Now he had a weapon.

He looked at Cavanaugh. "Listen—"

"How did you disable the alarm?" Cavanaugh cut him off.

"What alarm?" Sam's eyes widened with innocence. "Nothing beeped when I came in."

Philippe stepped away from her, reached to his lower back and came up with a gun.

Where had he gone that had required a weapon? Had Brant or Nick been able to follow him? The two men had begun watching the estate 24/7.

"Who are you?" The man motioned her toward Reese, standing between them and the door. "You," he said to Reese. "Put that down."

Faced with the gun, he had no other choice but to do as he'd been told. He put the candleholder on the floor by his feet, within easy reach. Not that a piece of scrap metal was a lot of help against a bullet.

Cavanaugh didn't miss anything. "Kick it over."

Reese kicked, but not too hard. The cast iron was pretty heavy in any case. The candleholder stopped halfway between the two of them.

"Philippe?" Sam kept up the charade. "Did something happen? What's going on?"

The man shook his head. "Game's up. Who do you work for?"

Reese measured the distance between them, swore silently and wished he hadn't let himself be talked out of the Beretta he had argued to bring. But Law and Tarasov thought it wasn't worth the risk, that their belongings might be searched, so in the end he had given in.

Man, he hated this mission. Give him an open confrontation with some guerilla group on the hillside any day of the week. He didn't like the idea of facing danger with a woman he cared for by his side. Give him his team and his weapons. Instead, he was here unarmed, worrying that any move he might make could put Sam's life in danger.

He needed to get Cavanaugh's gun away from him. But even if he had the man's gun, he couldn't shoot to kill. He couldn't shoot at all. They couldn't mess up with Philippe, their only link to Tsernyakov.

They would figure out what to do with Philippe later. Right now, they had to stabilize the situation.

Step one, he needed to distract the man. He glanced around the room and his gaze settled on the picture that, according to Sam, hid the room's safe. "We are here for the diadem," he said.

Cavanaugh narrowed his eyes.

If he called out to his goons downstairs it would be all over in minutes. But he seemed to believe that he had the situation well in hand. He paused for a long moment, looking from one to the other. "A lawyer and his jailbird friend— Yes, I know about that." He glanced at Sam. "Turning into cat burglars?" He ran his tongue over his teeth. "Tried this before, or am I the first unfortunate that you took for an idiot?"

The story did sound somewhat plausible, didn't it? Reese gave him an easy grin. "Everybody needs excitement and challenge in their lives."

"It wasn't like that, Philippe. The piece is insured. You are the richest man in the universe. It's just that we needed money." She did a good job making it look like she was about to cry. "When we came up with this stupid plan, I didn't know you. But it's been hard. Everything is different now."

Philippe laughed. "I didn't give you credit for the full extent of your talents. Very nice, Sam. But I'm not a casting agent. You can put the role-playing away." He shook his head. "How did you find out about the diadem? I bid through an agent."

"A client of mine bid on it, too," Reese improvised. "He was upset enough when he didn't win to investigate who did. He happened to mention it."

Cavanaugh took a few seconds to digest his words. "I thought we kept bumping into each other because you hunted affluent clients," he told Sam. "So the whole Savall business is bogus?" He sounded more fascinated than appalled. "All the women are in on this?"

"They think they are." Sam took over with a smile. She was quick on the uptake. She moved back toward Cavanaugh. "Hey, no harm done. You were smarter than us. You caught us. No hard feelings? Let's be friends. You might need us yet. Never know."

Reese let her handle the man. She had a better chance at charming Cavanaugh than he did.

"Shut up and don't move another centimeter." Cavanaugh turned the gun from Reese and pointed it at her, looking decidedly disinclined to be charmed.

He took a step toward Sam, taking his attention from Reese for a split second.

It was the break Reese had been waiting for.

Make it quick, make it quiet.

He launched himself at the man and brought him down as Sam flew for the door to close it, to make sure that the sound of the two men crashing to the floor wouldn't bring attention from down-stairs.

Cavanaugh held the gun firmly. Reese gripped his wrist, trying to stop him from aiming the weapon. He had to get it away from him. If the gun went off, Cavanaugh's men would be up here in seconds.

They rolled on the floor, grunting. Cavanaugh was in damn good shape.

Reese could see Sam in his peripheral vision, then she disappeared. Soon, he heard the sound of running water from the bathroom. Good—any-thing to mask the noise helped.

He kept pushing forward, pressing his body weight into Cavanaugh, not allowing him to take enough of a breath to call out. They were at an impasse, pretty well matched for strength.

He almost had the gun, but Philippe heaved. Reese's grip slipped. *Hang on. Hang on.* It wasn't enough to stop the man from shooting him or Sam. If the weapon was discharged at all, the sound would bring Philippe's goons running.

Reese brought his other hand up, which exposed his side. Cavanaugh immediately took advantage of that with a vicious stab of his elbow into Reese's ribs. He swallowed the pain.

Then Sam came out of nowhere and clunked Philippe in the back of the head with the candle-

stick. The man reeled enough from the blow so
Reese could bring the heel of his hand hard into
his chin, smack his head back and knock him out.

He rolled to the side and gobbled some air.

"Thanks," he told Sam without taking his attention off the man next to him. He grabbed the gun
away from Philippe and tucked it behind his back
then looked up at her, grinning.

Sam grinned back, but didn't stop to bask in
their success. She snatched a pillow off the bed,
stripped it and ripped the cover. "Let's secure him
before he wakes."

"Good thinking."

He lifted Cavanaugh's head from the floor so
she could gag him. He was already coming to.
Reese grabbed the leftover fabric, made two strips
and bound his hands and feet.

Philippe looked from Reese to Sam with a
clouded expression at first, then his gaze widened
as the events of the past few minutes came back
to him and his eyes began to burn with hate. He
was growling from behind the gag.

"Quiet." Reese pointed the gun at him.

"What are we going to do with him?" Sam
glanced toward the door.

Good question. Their undercover mission was
over as they knew it, their cover blown and the
rules of the game completely changed from here

on out. This wasn't supposed to happen. Whatever came next, Cavanaugh could not be allowed to establish contact with Tsernyakov. "We'll have to kidnap him."

Except that his sudden disappearance would make Tsernyakov suspicious. They still needed to get close enough to T to figure out where exactly the attack was going down and how. They needed that information to stop whatever evildoing was in the making.

Reese gave the gun to Sam then went into the bathroom. He took out his phone, dialed Brant and told him what had just transpired at the mansion.

Brant swore. "Maybe we can turn him." He paused.

They both knew how unlikely that was.

"We'll come up with a solution," he went on. "I have an idea, but I can't come to you. One of you have to come in."

He was about to respond, when a knock sounded on the suite's door. He clicked off the phone.

"Sir?" one of Cavanaugh's men was saying.

Sam gave an exaggerated squeal.

"Sir?"

"He's in the bathtub." Sam giggled.

Reese made some splashing sounds with his

hand, in case it could be heard over the running water.

"I didn't mean to disturb," the voice apologized.

Reese walked out of the bathroom and looked at Sam. They held their breath and each other's gazes for a few endless seconds.

"I think he's gone. You can turn off the water," she whispered. "What did Brant say?"

Nothing good, he thought. He didn't want to be separated from her just now. The situation was too dangerous. But he had to trust that she could handle herself.

He walked over to her and kissed her gently on the mouth. How could anyone be this sweet and this tough at the same time? She was going to be his undoing for sure.

"You're wanted at the office," he said.

SAM SKIPPED down the stairs and flashed a smile— the kind Eva usually doled out—at the two men in the front foyer.

"Could someone bring around my car?"

They just looked at her. One of them glanced up the stairs. Were they waiting for Cavanaugh's permission that she could leave?

"Philippe got some superimportant call." She rolled her eyes. "Since it looks like he'll be a while, he told me to go get something *special…*"

She looked away bashfully for effect. "That we've been talking about."

The taller of the two men walked out the door. She flashed another smile at the one who was staying, then followed.

Her car was up in the front driveway in another minute or two. She kept an eye on the rearview mirror as she pulled the Celica through the gate. Roberto was getting into one of the black BMWs that always stood at the ready. Was it too much to hope that he was just going to the grocery store? A couple of turns confirmed her suspicions. She *was* being followed.

Time to get rid of the man.

She ran a red light. So did he.

She had to get rid of the man without him realizing that she was trying to get rid of him. If he got suspicious that something was up, he might call back to the mansion to warn Philippe about her. And Philippe definitely couldn't come to the phone right now.

She skipped in and out of traffic, but apparently Roberto had plenty of experience at shadowing people because he stuck behind her. Traffic being what it was, she couldn't outrace him. She turned down an alley behind a row of restaurants and dodged garbage containers. A truck was coming off a loading dock. That could be just the break she needed. She timed it, stepped on the gas just as they were next to each other. The next second, the truck rolled out into the alley and blocked the way behind her.

"See you later, Roberto." She grinned.

Her sense of accomplishment lasted for about half a mile. At the next major intersection, by some major bad stroke of luck, she found herself side by side with the man at the red light.

She didn't have time for this. Sam clenched her teeth and considered her options. Then the solution popped into her head.

She drove to a large shopping center that was only a few blocks from Savall's office and weaved through the three-story parking garage. Roberto kept right behind her. Fine. She got out of the car and headed for the elevator. He couldn't very well get on it with her. He would know that she would recognize him and realize that she was being followed. At least, she hoped he had as much logic as that.

She got off on the main level and found herself in a light-filled atrium that buzzed with shoppers. She plunged into the crowd. Getting lost here shouldn't be hard. She'd spent plenty of cold winter days at malls in her youth, dodging mall security with the inventiveness of a desperate teenager.

She was going through the food court when she

glanced back and saw Roberto get off the elevator. He looked around, annoyed. She stepped behind a pretzel stand before he could spot her. Then, when he was looking in the other direction, she took off toward the entrance of a major department store, glass cases stocked with perfume and cosmetics. *So much for Roberto.* She grinned. Never try to outrace a woman at a mall.

She crossed the department store and took the escalator to the next level where she left the store and went back to the main bank of elevators. In less than five minutes she was back in her car. In ten more, she was parking in front of the office.

"Nobody followed you?" Gina asked when she walked through the door.

"Lost him," she said as if it were no big deal.

"Knew you could." Gina grinned.

"Is everything okay?" Anita was walking toward her.

"Will be if you have a solution for me."

Brant was coming out of his office with a small paper bag in his hand and held it out. "Here it is."

She took it and glanced in. A syringe and a vial. "What is it?"

"A drug used by diabetics. When used improperly it causes hypoglycemia that mimics the symptoms of a stroke."

"Will it kill him?"

Could she do it? Could she shove a needle into a man's arm and watch him die, even if he was a criminal? She had thought about what would happen if things got rough, considered the possibilities when she had signed on to the mission. But back then it seemed a far-off possibility. Faced with it now, she was drowning in self-doubt.

Shooting back at someone who was shooting at you was a different matter. But to inject Cavanaugh with poison while he was tied and gagged… "I'm not sure—"

But Brant shook his head. "He'll be fine. Don't worry. I want him to stand trial for all the dirty business he's been conducting on the island."

"But if Tsernyakov talks to Philippe before we get to Tsernyakov, the whole operation will be ruined. If T thinks we are on to him— The deal could be canceled. Or worse, the date of the attack could be brought up, leaving us no time to stop it."

"Why don't you sit down and we'll run through this," Brant said and told her about the plan.

"I'M GLAD YOU can come." Tsernyakov scanned a handful of printouts as he talked on the phone.

His office looked like a hurricane had swept through it. Files lay on the floor, waiting to be sorted into boxes; three giant garbage cans spilled over with what he had selected for his secretary to shred. He was packing up, getting ready to move out.

Too bad. He liked this office in Saint Petersburg with the view of the river in the distance. The big windows let the sunshine through in the morning, putting him into an instant good mood as soon as he plopped into his bloodred executive leather chair, a gift from a friend. He liked how high up he was, how he could look over most of the buildings, watch the people and the cars on the street. His empire.

He was going to miss this view.

"You are my most important client," Cal said on the other end of the line. "And family comes first, anyway. I'm not going to forget what you've done for me."

Cal Spencer, his second cousin who lived in England and owned a slew of strategically placed warehouses, was, indeed, indebted to him. His connections had saved Cal from some nasty insider-trading charges not long ago.

Now most of Cal's warehouses stored Tsernyakov's bootie, plus basic essentials he was stockpiling for after the virus had been released. He was determined to come out on top once all was said and done.

And he'd decided that he would keep Cal. He was a useful sort of chap, as the British said, and he was family. He was a good businessman. He wasn't afraid of a little foul play, as proven by that unfortunate incident with the London Stock Exchange.

"The island is fine. It won't be all about work. You can bring a girlfriend if you'd like."

His invitation was for a prolonged visit to his small private island in the South Pacific under the pretext of him needing Cal's advice for starting up a shipping-and-storage business in the region. Cal seemed happy to provide his expertise, pay back the favor he owed. He had no idea he was about to receive another gift, his life. On the island, cut off from the world, he would be safe.

"Don't have a girl, I'm sad to say."

"Even better, there'll be plenty of them there. Nice Russian girls, too." He was even considering inviting the four women of Savall, Ltd. Cavanaugh just couldn't shut up about them. And he did need their money-laundering services; he had a few small fortunes he needed to move before the widespread collapse of the banking system in the West.

The ladies of Savall, Ltd. would make a useful addition to the group of gorgeous women he had already invited to the island. Alexandra was charming. She was all he had hoped and more. Pliant, eager to please, full of youthful enthusiasm. She looked up to him, and the open adoration felt wonderful. And she was grateful to him, so gratifyingly grateful for everything.

He had already sent her to his ranch in the Andes where he would ride out the storm. He didn't want to be on the island with the people he'd decided to save. He wasn't sure what their first reaction would be when they found out he'd had a hand in the coming disaster. And they would be suspicious; they weren't stupid. They wouldn't buy that it was sheer luck that left his interests unscathed. They would grieve for their families and blame him. Hell, he couldn't save everyone.

The virus wasn't that bad, anyway. It wouldn't kill everyone, just cull the weak.

Once the men and women he'd chosen settled down and accepted the way things were, once they realized what they owed him and that there was no way out, he would tell them what he expected of them. In a couple of months, they would be ready to do his bidding.

Chapter Eleven

Sam walked without hurry, smiled at the guards who were now lounging outside the front door. Everything looked normal. She wouldn't let the relief show.

"Philippe ask for me yet?" She twirled her handbag, as if her heart wasn't beating a mile a minute.

One of the men shook his head.

She just sashayed into the house.

Roberto was in the living room, watching TV, the only guard in there. He looked up as she came in, and a dark little gleam entered his eyes. "Come keep me company." He patted the couch next to him.

"Philippe is waiting for me." She headed for the stairs.

He was up, moving faster than she would have expected of him, cutting off her passage, grabbing for her wrist. "What's the hurry? You think you're too good for me?"

The smell of alcohol hit her. She tried to tug her hand free, but he held tight. "We were discussing business. He is going to look for me. I told him I wouldn't be long."

He sneered at that. "You can discuss business with me first." He yanked her hard against him.

If she called out for Reese, the men in front of the door outside would hear her, too, and rush in.

"Later. First let me finish what I started upstairs."

That seemed to anger Roberto. He held her even tighter. "Philippe must get first taste of everything. Is that it? You don't know how sick of him I am."

"You had a little to drink. Don't do anything you might regret later." She held his gaze. "You know how he is."

But Roberto had obviously passed the point where he could clearly recall just how tough Cavanaugh could be with employees who displeased him. "Come with me for a second." He leaned closer, and she held her breath. "Give me a little something to convince me to wait for the rest."

Oh God. This was the absolute worst time for him to go crazy like this. He was tugging her toward the door under the stairs, one of the doors Cavanaugh had never shown her. If she went with Roberto, she might find something important.

Also, she could fight him off behind closed doors, which she didn't want to do here for fear that the sounds of struggle would alert the men outside.

She let him drag her behind him.

The room they entered was maybe fifteen by fifteen, with a cot and a table and a small TV. Did the guards take turns crashing here? She didn't get a chance to have a better look around. Roberto pushed her against the wall roughly, knocking the air out of her lungs.

She pushed her shoulder bag out of the way. The idiot was going to break the vial with the drug in it if she wasn't careful.

"Later," she said as forcefully as she could and shoved against him.

He didn't budge an inch. "Now. I told you, it won't take long."

"Get off me." She struggled for air, which seemed to be in short supply all of a sudden.

He crushed against her, shoving his mouth against hers, his full weight pinning her to the wall. Panic rose from within. She banged her fists into his shoulders and twisted her head wildly. "Stop it!"

She fought against him with everything Nick Tarasov had taught her at Quantico, but he was too heavy to shove off. She butted her forehead into his nose with all her strength. He gave an outraged growl and moved back an inch or two, just to slam her into the wall again.

She struggled to knee him in the groin, but he was standing too close for that. She couldn't bring up her knees. Panic pushed her to fight without thought, to claw her way away from him, but after a few seconds she realized that wasn't going to work. She was seriously outpowered. She had to calm down and use her brains.

She went slack as he put a hand between them and squeezed her breast until it hurt. Then she made herself lower her hand between them, as well, and reached for the buckle of his belt.

"Knew I could convince you. You're a smart girl." Roberto slobbered into her neck. "I'm a big man. You'll see. Much bigger than Philippe."

Her hand hesitated on the buckle. She drew in some air then tugged on the metal. He moved back a little to give her room. She'd been hoping for that.

Sam brought up her right knee as hard as she could, then, as he folded, she brought the other knee into his chin.

"You bitch," he groaned, going down hard. And still he wouldn't give up. He was grabbing for her ankle.

Dark memories rushed to immobilize her with fear as his fat fingers closed around her, bruising her skin. She dragged herself away, her body trembling. Roberto was coming up already. "I wasn't going to hurt you, but you're going to pay for this." He lunged at her.

No, not again. Not ever again. She wasn't a victim. She was strong. She was a survivor. Reese's words came to her and held back the darkness. She could win over Roberto if she found a way to beat back the memories that gripped her inside, making her stiff with fear.

She was a survivor.

She hooked her leg behind Roberto's as he was clinging to her. The man went down a second time, with a bone-rattling crash. Wasn't as quick to get up again. There must have been some truth to the bigger-they-are-the-harder-they-fall adage.

"I'll kill you for this," he hissed between his teeth.

"You as much as look at me again and you'll deal with Philippe."

"You think I'm afraid of him?" he boasted as he struggled to stand. "I've been with him for ten years. He tosses whores like you aside every day." He spat the words at her.

She was at the door already, but a second too late. He had a gun out and pointed at her.

"You get back."

All she could think of was that she couldn't die

here. Reese needed her upstairs. Her team needed her to come through with the mission. She took one cautious step toward Roberto then another.

"Look, things shouldn't have gone this far. I lost my head. I don't want to get Philippe mad. My company can't afford to lose the business, that's all. Just let me go up there for a while. I'll come right back." She stopped just outside of reach.

"Get down here."

She moved forward slowly, another few inches.

His hand shot out and grabbed her, pulled her down hard on her knees. He was sitting with his knees up and his legs spread. He pulled her closer and put the gun in the middle of her forehead. "Forget Philippe. I'm the damn boss now. You do what I say you do."

She had come eye to eye with death before, but it wasn't one of those things a person got used to. Adrenaline pumped through her blood, and mind-numbing fear, making it impossible to focus on anything but the cold metal pressed against her skin.

"I'll do what you want."

"Damn right you will." He reached up with his free hand and pulled her tank top up to reveal her abdomen. "Take it off."

She reached up with trembling fingers and pulled the thin material over her breasts. He seemed too impatient to wait any longer. He shoved her to the floor and turned to fall on her, lowering the gun in the process.

He was with his back to the door now, didn't notice as Reese quietly came in. The fury of hell was in his eyes as he took a step forward. Sam sent him a look of desperate pleading. *Stay.*

The mission was more important than she was. Reese couldn't blow his cover. He wasn't supposed to be in the mansion. Philippe's goons by the front door would have never let him in. If Roberto saw him, he'd know something was up.

He moved forward anyway.

Roberto lifted his head a little, maybe hearing some noise. Sam didn't give him time to turn around. She twisted and slammed her elbow into his temple. Then, as he went limp, she grabbed the gun and hit him over the head with it for good measure.

Reese was there to roll him off her.

"I could handle him."

"So I see." His face was dark as he watched her, then in the next second crushed her to him. "Sorry, sorry." He pulled away then. "I didn't mean to."

"No." She burrowed back into his arms. She needed the comfort he offered. Her only regret was that they had to rush.

She pulled away after a few seconds. "Cavanaugh?"

"He's tied up as best as I could, but we'd better go, anyway, before someone goes looking for him," he said. "You got a plan for what to do with him?"

She picked up her purse from the floor. "I have an excellent plan." She gave him a brief update then looked out the door. The living room was still empty.

They left the guards' room and stole up the stairs, watching their backs the whole time.

"How did you know to come and look for me?" she asked when they were inside the room and she could see that Philippe was still there and everything was okay, for now.

"Saw you arrive through the window. Wondered what was going on when you didn't come up."

"Thanks."

"He was lucky you dealt with him. I wouldn't have been that gentle."

The cold anger in his voice was scary, making her wonder just what he would have done to Roberto if she hadn't managed on her own.

Cavanaugh growled around the cloth in his mouth. He was probably swearing at them.

"Did he say anything new?" It was great that they had a date, but in itself it was little more than nothing. They needed a lot more information than that if the attack was to be preempted.

"No. And I did try. I don't think he knows much beyond the date. You're bleeding."

"What?" It took her a second to register that last part.

He was holding her arm. Sure enough, blood trickled down her skin.

She had slammed against several things downstairs, but she didn't realize in the excitement that something had torn her skin. Now that she saw the wound, however, she immediately began to feel the pain, too. Not for long.

"Give me your tank top." He drew a finger along the wound as he examined it. "I don't think it's dangerously deep."

Maybe. But he sure seemed dangerously close. She felt embarrassed all of a sudden about pulling her tank top over her head, and how insane was that? She had a bra on, no different than the dozens of times he'd seen her in a bikini.

The way he studiously avoided looking at anything but the wound told her that he, too, was feeling some of the warm tension that sprung to life between them. He wrapped her arm in the soft material, nice and snug to stanch the flow of blood. Then he strode to Cavanaugh's closet, pulled out an island-print shirt and handed it to her.

She slipped into the shirt, eager to put that thin barrier between them.

"This shouldn't make anyone suspicious," he said.

He was right. Being in a state of semiundress would be natural for a woman in Cavanaugh's suite, and the shirt covered the makeshift bandage.

Philippe was growling something from behind the gag. Reese walked toward him.

She followed and pulled the paper bag out of her purse. Time to get on with the show. "Hold his arm."

Cavanaugh thrashed when he saw the syringe.

"This is not going to kill you," she told him.

Apparently, he didn't believe her. He threw his weight forward and crashed his chair to the floor. They had to have heard that downstairs.

"His arm." She put her weight on him to hold him down.

Reese finally got his arm. "Hurry."

Philippe howled around the gag as she injected him. Then he began to shake, his eyes rolling back in his head.

People were coming up the stairs.

"Quick." Reese took off the gag as she shoved the syringe into her purse.

They untied him from the chair. Reese bunched the straps into his pants pocket before dropping and rolling under the bed.

A knock sounded at the door. "Are you all right, *monsieur?*"

Sam rubbed the tie marks around Philippe's wrists and face. There. Barely visible now. The drug was turning him red, anyway.

"Help me!" she screamed.

The door burst open and three men poured in, all with gun in hand.

"A stroke." She shook Philippe. "I think he had a stroke. He was having trouble moving his arm. Said he had a headache. Then he fell down."

The guns were put away as one of the guys called for an ambulance.

"You'd better go back to your room," another one told her, kneeling down to Philippe. "Call the front gate to make sure they let the ambulance through." He barked the order at one of the others.

Roberto skulked in, rubbing his head, and stared daggers at her. He would go after her again if he got half the chance.

It didn't matter. He couldn't do anything now. "Wake up, honey. Wake up." She wouldn't let go of Philippe's hand, doing her best to appear hysterical.

"You two take anything?" the other security guy asked, his eyes narrowing as he watched her.

She shook her head. Looked away. "I told him about something new I tried and he wanted a sample, but— I just got back. He was still on the phone. He was angry with somebody— And then he just dropped." She wailed.

The third guy came over and dropped next to Philippe, put a hand on the man's chest and started CPR.

"He's breathing. He's breathing." She put a hand out to stop him and sobbed for good measure. The idiot was going to kill him. Giving CPR to someone who didn't need it could actually stop their heart. She'd watched plenty of hospital soaps in the can.

The guy moved back.

"I'll walk you back to your room," Roberto told her as she stood. There seemed to be a slight limp to his step as he moved around.

She pressed a hand to her chest, swallowed. "Oh God. I think I'm going to be sick." She sat down and pulled up her knees, put her head between them.

"Breathe deep," the other man said, and it looked as if, for the moment, he was willing to give up on the idea of evicting her. "We should at least put him in the bed."

And for a minute or two that kept them busy.

Then, finally, the ambulance arrived, the crew coming up the stairs and into the room with the stretcher.

"Could you give me name and date of birth?" Anita, in an EMT uniform, was holding a clipboard.

One of his men supplied the information.

"Any medical conditions?"

"None."

"Drug allergies?"

"None. Isn't he too young for a stroke?"

Carly was taking his blood pressure and feeling his pulse. "Average age for stroke is fifty-six." For once her knowledge of odd trivia came in handy, making her look like she was a true professional.

Cavanaugh was fifty-one if the data the FBI had on him was correct.

"Can't you do more to help him?" the security guard demanded.

"We're working on it," Gina soothed him. "Please, let's give the man some air. Everyone who is not working on him, please leave the room."

"I think I'm going to faint," Sam said weakly.

"Okay." Gina went over to her and took her pulse. "She stays. Everyone else, please get out. You can watch from the door."

The men did as she said, and as soon as they were out, Gina and Anita positioned themselves to give cover to Carly, who moved toward the nightstand. With a couple of swift moves, she had the hard drive out of Cavanaugh's laptop and a blank one put in.

Gina started an IV on Cavanaugh. She'd been a volunteer medic during her police academy days.

"Looks like a stroke," Anita told the men. "We are taking him to Georgetown Municipal Hospital. If someone wants to come in with him, they can follow the ambulance. Please bring his insurance card and ID."

"What about her?" Carly checked Sam's pupils like a pro.

"Better keep an eye on her for a couple of hours. Might as well take her in, too."

Roberto glared at her.

She glared back. Like hell he was going to intimidate her.

"Can you walk, ma'am?" Anita came to help her up.

Gina and Carly put Cavanaugh on the stretcher and headed for the door. Anita escorted Sam behind them.

"And now?" Sam asked once the ambulance door was closed behind them.

"He'll be in critical care. He can be visited only by one person at a time for one hour each day. For that hour he'll be sedated. Brant has a doctor at the hospital who will make sure no mishaps occur."

"Reese doesn't think he knows anything about the attack beyond the date."

Carly pulled a small bag of doughnuts from her medical case and offered it around. "Being nervous makes me hungry," she said.

"We've got some good news," Anita told Sam, grinning.

"What?" Sam asked.

"Just after you left, we got a call from a potential new client who was apparently referred to us by Cavanaugh," Anita said.

That definitely called for one of Carly's doughnuts.

Gina took one, too. "He wants to meet us on his private island early next week to discuss the possibilities of us working for him full-time. He's offering an exclusive contract, basically."

"We can't do that. We have to stay in business as is and try to attract Tsernyakov." And they were dangerously close to running out of time.

"The island is owned by a Russian media mogul. On paper. In reality, he's never been there. The local rumor is that it's used by some hotshot from the Russian mob."

"So?"

"The ships we have satellite images of that docked there for the last couple of days are for the most registered to companies we had listed as suspicious for either doing business with or actually belonging to Tsernyakov."

The air stopped in Sam's lungs. "You think this is it?"

The women nodded. "We did it."

They'd been working toward that goal for months, but now that it was here, she could barely believe that they had succeeded.

They had a date. Plus, they had Cavanaugh in their power. Interrogating him should bring more information, as well. And they had attracted Tsernyakov's attention, finally, just as they had set out to do. She had done her part, hadn't failed the others or the mission, or herself. That thought kept her happy all the way to the office where she was distracted by other things.

Brant, Nick, David and Reese were waiting for them. Sam watched some byplay between the brothers as they stood side by side. David looked a lot smaller and a lot less handsome all of a sudden.

Reese must have sensed her watching because he turned and looked straight at her. Smiled.

She felt a responding smile tugging at her lips. Her heart started doing a crazy little dance. She was so far gone it was pitiful.

She was in love with Reese Moretti.

She sure hadn't seen that coming. He didn't look like his usual confident self, either. He had a goofy expression on his face as he watched her.

Maybe they would meet again someday, years from now, when both of them were ready. Right. Her luck didn't work that way and—

She stopped herself midthought.

She met Reese, didn't she?

Maybe her luck was changing. Or maybe she should take luck into her own two hands. She flashed him a hopeful grin.

Chapter Twelve

"You have to leave already?" Sam watched as Reese packed his duffel bag, leaving behind the "lawyer clothes" he had borrowed from his brother.

They had spent the ride from the office to her apartment in silence, Reese so deep in thought she couldn't budge him out of it. Maybe he was switching gears, focusing on his next mission.

"I have the information I needed from the FBI. It gives me the rough location of the people who most likely took my client. My team is already on their way there. I'm flying in tonight."

He wore blue jeans and a black T-shirt, the set of his mouth as grim as when he had arrived.

"I don't know how to thank you. Without you—"

He looked at her and his face lightened a fraction. "You would have done just fine. You're a hell of a lot stronger than you give yourself credit for."

She shook her head. If only he knew. She was about to fall into his arms and beg him to stay.

"About—" She wanted to talk about what had happened between them beyond the mission, but couldn't find the words. What if he'd forgotten it already? What if it meant nothing to him?

He stopped what he was doing. "I wasn't playing with you. I want you to know that. I wish things were different for the both of us."

She swallowed.

He was so gloriously handsome and fierce-looking just now. She stepped closer without meaning to. "Me, too."

"You are an extraordinary woman. You don't have to rush anything."

Was that desire in his eyes? "I'm not." She took another step.

"When the time is right, when the man is right, it will come naturally." He scratched an eyebrow and gave her a tight smile. "He'll be one lucky bastard, that's for sure."

What did he think he was doing, talking about other men? She wasn't interested in anyone but him.

"And if I want you?" She couldn't believe she was brave enough to say that.

He went still. "You don't have to settle for me. I can't give you what you want, the quiet life, the being there with you day in, day out, the security."

"Maybe that's not what I want. Not right now, anyway."

He looked surprised. "But that's how it should be," he said with conviction.

"Maybe that's what you want, then."

He paused. "I know what I want. I love my job. My clients need me."

"How about what you need?"

"I'm no longer sure." He gave her a rueful grin. "Okay, so I'll reevaluate. It's not going to happen overnight, though."

"I didn't ask for anything."

"Point taken. But I want to give you everything." He held her gaze. "I want you."

His words drummed through her bloodstream. She moved another few inches in his direction. Just a foot or two separated them now. There was so much he didn't know about her. She owed him the truth, no matter how scared she was of rejection, even if he would walk away when he realized who and what she was.

"I tell people I don't remember anything before I came to live on the streets, but I do."

The muscles in his face tightened.

"I remember everything," she whispered. And all of a sudden she felt the sudden need to talk about it, talk to *him* about it. That urge caught her off guard. For years she'd done everything possible to block out her past.

"You want to tell me?" He closed the distance between them and put his arms around her.

She pressed against his body, the solid strength of him. Then she began to speak and lay her soul bare to him.

"He can't hurt you now. None of those things can. You've made it through," he said when she was done. "You are more than the memories of your past."

They were sitting on the sofa, Reese holding her in his arms.

"I know. So are you." And when he looked at her with questions in his eyes, she said, "Natalie wasn't your fault."

He took a slow breath and swallowed. "Hell, I've carried that around so long now, I don't know if I can let it go."

"I've been thinking," she said. "I think it's okay to remember, but we don't have to feel guilty. Either of us."

"I'll try."

He lifted a hand to caress her face and she tilted her mouth for a kiss. He took it and kissed her with care at first then with heat. Enough heat to melt the memories away.

"But what we have— It doesn't work like this," he said when he pulled away after a long while.

"What doesn't?" From where she was sitting, it had been working just fine.

"It was a man who broke something in you in some way. Giving your body to another man is not going to heal it. Only you can. In here." He touched a hand to her heart.

She thought about that. What was in her heart? It used to be filled with fear. Now it was filled with Reese.

"That's not why I wanted to kiss you," she said.

He drew up an eyebrow.

"Reese, I—"

He put two fingers to her mouth. "Don't say anything. I'm half in love with you already. Don't make this harder than it has to be."

Her heart thrilled. "I've never known anyone like you."

"You don't need anyone like me."

It was her turn to put her eyebrows in action. "Can I decide what I need?"

"I travel a lot. You'd be alone a lot."

"I'm alone all the time now." He didn't seem to have a response to that, so she went on. "You know what I learned in the last couple of years? That the planets rarely align to make everything just perfect for reaching everlasting happiness. You have to grab the half chances, the bits and pieces and run with it." She'd rather have him in her life from time to time than not at all.

"When did you get so wise?"

She smiled.

"I will get out of this business someday, you know," he added. "This isn't something anyone can do forever. People who do this job have to be at the top of their game."

It wasn't as if she was ready for marriage and a family at this second, anyway. She wanted to go back to college, she wanted to discover the world and all she had missed in it. She was twenty-two. He was a man worth waiting for.

"On average, I'm home a week every other month." He kissed her again.

"We'll just have to make the best of it," she said when they came up for air.

"But this current job shouldn't take more than a week or two, now that we have a location."

She ran her hand under his shirt.

He caught it and held it to his heart. "Is this truly what you want?"

"I want to live. Really live. I want to learn. I want time to figure out what I want from life. But one thing I do know for sure. I do want you to be part of it."

He crushed her to him, tight. "How did I get so lucky? I have a condo in Boston. I would love it if you lived there with me." He looked into her eyes. "I promise to give you lots of space. We'll take it as slow as you need." He paused for a grin. "Free lifetime supply of cotton candy."

She considered him for a moment. "I want to go to school and I want to work with street kids."

"Plenty of colleges in Boston. Plenty of disadvantaged children, too."

She closed her eyelids for a few seconds and let herself imagine what that would be like. Real living. Learning. Productive. Making up for the mistakes of the past. Reese in her life. The wonder of it all misted her eyes.

"Okay, there's something I haven't been completely honest about," he said.

Her eyes popped open, all her insecurities surfacing in a surge. She was prepared for the worst in a split second, and hated that she had so much practice that her instincts would kick in with the speed of light.

"When I said I'm half in love with you—" he caressed her jawline with a thumb "—I might have been hanging on to some macho image of myself. Can't-be-brought-down-with-a-single-look kind of stuff, you know?"

She shook her head as heat spread from his touch. She had no idea what he was talking about.

"I'm pretty sure I'm in love with you all the way," he said.

She lowered herself to the couch and somehow drew him with her.

"How do I know when I'm in love? I don't have any practice at this," she said.

"Me, neither. We'll figure it out. We make a damn good team."

"I can't imagine you not being in my life. Is that love?"

He grinned. "I'll take that for starters."

"I've never felt as alive and happy as I do when I'm with you."

He put his arms around her and nuzzled her ear. "Keep going."

"I feel like I'll go mad if I can't touch you. Or if you don't touch me."

"That's very, very good." He touched his lips to hers, gentle and warm, and kissed her until she was so full of love and desire for him that she was bursting with it.

She realized she was gathered in his lap, in the circle of his arms, but it didn't feel restrictive, didn't raise a single alarm. Just the opposite, she felt loved and protected.

She leaned back and pulled him with her until they were lying side by side. Her couch might have been the most ugly piece of furniture on the island, but it was wide enough for two, an advantage that made up for a slew of sins right now.

She looked into his gaze, which was filled with love and desire, and thought she could just stay like that forever, have him look at her like that. She was wrong. In a few moments, she wanted more.

She cupped his face and kissed him. That would satisfy her until the end of time, she thought, but soon she found she was wrong again. Her lips wanted to wander and discover the strong line of his jaw, his cheek, his neck. There she came against a roadblock in the form of his T-shirt.

"Would you mind taking this off?"

His gaze burned hers as he did so.

And all of a sudden her mouth went dry at the proximity of the wide expanse of his chest, the flat muscles, the heat that emanated from him. It wasn't the first time she'd seen him shirtless; they've even been in bed like this before. But they were on a mission, focusing—or pretending to be focusing—on other things. There were no more pretenses between them now.

She lifted a hand to his chest and laid it flat against him, glanced up when he sucked in air with a sharp sound.

"Not complaining," he said quickly, but his voice did sound strangled.

She went back to exploring him, tentatively touching his nipple first with her fingertip then her tongue.

He rolled onto his back and gave her free rein.

She was touching him and was aware that it had an effect on him—okay, a strong effect. But what was strange was that it also had an equally strong effect on her. As if the fire in him ran up her arm and into her body to fill it up. Heat waves and tingling. She liked it. Wanted it. But still, she wanted more.

She loved the strength of the muscles under the soft skin, the smattering of silky hair, the width of his shoulders, the flat plane of his stomach.

She put a hand to his fly, ready to pop buttons, and undid them one by one, until she could see the stretching cotton briefs. She ran a finger along the waistband.

"You'd better not touch…um…below that line." His voice was scratchy. "Give me a moment to recover here."

The power she had over him was heady. His self-control—he hadn't touched her yet—making her fall in love with him all over again.

"But I can look?" She smiled up at him.

He groaned. "Okay. Go ahead and look."

He lifted his hips so she could tug the jeans down, then helped her get rid of them along with his underwear. He lay before her in his full naked glory, so beautiful it took her breath away.

And all of a sudden, she wanted to feel his skin against hers, every inch of it. She tugged off her shirt and the bra underneath and reached for her shorts, looked up at him. He fisted his hands and folded them under his head, a fierce concentration on his face.

She understood what he was doing, why he wasn't helping. He wanted to make sure this was what she wanted, that she did only as much as she wanted. He gave her complete control of the situation, complete control over his magnificent body.

She shrugged out of the shorts, feeling shy all of a sudden, snuggling up to him to cover her body against his.

"You're beautiful," he said.

She burrowed into his heat.

"We don't have to do this. Go any further. If you don't want— What I mean is, I'll wait as long as you need. It doesn't have to be today."

"I think I'd die if it isn't." The words slipped from her lips.

He grinned. "Okay. Pretty much, me, too."

"We are too young to meet an untimely end like that," she joked, feeling lighthearted all of a sudden.

"Go ahead then." He brought his mouth down for a kiss. "Save us both."

And she did.

* * * * *

Look for the conclusion of
Dana Marton's Mission: Redemption *series*
next month when INTIMATE DETAILS
debuts in Harlequin Intrigue!

Welcome to cowboy country...

Turn the page for a sneak preview of
TEXAS BABY
by
Kathleen O'Brien
An exciting new title from
Harlequin Superromance for everyone
who loves stories about the West.

Harlequin Superromance—
Where life and love weave together in
emotional and unforgettable ways.

CHAPTER ONE

CHASE TRANSFERRED his gaze to the road and identified a foreign spot on the horizon. A car. Almost half a mile away, where the straight, tree-lined drive met the public road. He could tell it was coming too fast, but judging the speed of a vehicle moving straight toward you was tricky.

It wasn't until it was about two hundred yards away that he realized the driver must be drunk...or crazy. Or both.

The guy was going maybe sixty. On a private drive, out here in ranch country, where kids or horses or tractors or stupid chickens might come darting out any minute, that was criminal. Chase straightened from his comfortable slouch and waved his hands.

"Slow down, you fool," he called out. He took the porch steps quickly and began walking fast down the driveway.

The car veered oddly, from one lane to another,

then up onto the slight rise of the thick green spring grass. It just barely missed the fence.

"Slow down, damn it!"

He couldn't see the driver, and he didn't recognize this automobile. It was small and old, and couldn't have cost much even when it was new. It was probably white, but now it needed either a wash or a new paint job or both.

"Damn it, what's wrong with you?"

At the last minute, he had to jump away, because the idiot behind the wheel clearly wasn't going to turn to avoid a collision. He couldn't believe it. The car kept coming, finally slowing a little, but it was too late.

Still going about thirty miles an hour, it slammed into the large, white-brick pillar that marked the front boundaries of the house. The pillar wasn't going to give an inch, so the car had to. The front end folded up like a paper fan.

It seemed to take forever for the car to settle, as if the trauma happened in slow motion, reverberating from the front to the back of the car in ripples of destruction. The front windshield suddenly seemed to ice over with lethal bits of glassy frost. Then the side windows exploded.

The front driver's door wrenched open, as if the car wanted to expel its contents. Metal buckled hideously. Small pieces, like hubcaps and mirrors, skipped and ricocheted insanely across the oyster-shell driveway.

Finally, everything was still. Into the silence, a plume of steam shot up like a geyser, smelling of rust and heat. Its snakelike hiss almost smothered the low, agonized moan of the driver.

Chase's anger had disappeared. He didn't feel anything but a dull sense of disbelief. Things like this didn't happen in real life. Not in his life. Maybe the sun had actually put him to sleep....

But he was already kneeling beside the car. The driver was a woman. The frosty glass-ice of the windshield was dotted with small flecks of blood. She must have hit it with her head, because just below her hairline a red liquid was seeping out. He touched it. He tried to wipe it away before it reached her eyebrow, though of course, that made no sense at all. Her eyes were shut.

Was she conscious? Did he dare move her? Her dress was covered in glass, and the metal of the car was sticking out lethally in all the wrong places.

Then he remembered, with an intense relief, that every good medical man in the county was here, just behind the house, drinking his champagne. He found his phone and paged Trent.

The woman moaned again.

Alive, then. Thank God for that.

He saw Trent coming toward him, starting out at a lope, but quickly switching to a full run.

"Get Dr. Marchant," Chase called. "Don't bother with 911."

Trent didn't take long to assess the situation. A fraction of a second, and he began pulling out his cell phone and running toward the house.

The yelling seemed to have roused the woman. She opened her eyes. They were blue and clouded with pain and confusion.

"Chase," she said.

His breath stalled. His head pulled back. "What?"

Her only answer was another moan, and he wondered if he had imagined the word. He reached around her and put his arm behind her shoulders. She was tiny. Probably petite by nature, but surely way too thin. He could feel her shoulder blades pushing against her skin, as fragile as the wishbone in a turkey.

She seemed to have passed out, so he put his other arm under her knees and lifted her out. He tried to avoid the jagged metal, but her skirt caught on a piece and the tearing sound seemed to wake her again.

"No," she said. "Please."

"I'm just trying to help," he said. "It's going to be all right."

She seemed profoundly distressed. She wriggled in his arms, and she was so weak, like a broken bird. It made him feel too big and brutish. And intrusive. As if touching her this way, his bare hands against the warm skin behind her knees, were somehow a transgression.

He wished he could be more delicate. But he smelled gasoline, and he knew it wasn't safe to leave her here.

Finally he heard the sound of voices, as guests began to run around the side of the house, alerted by Trent. Dr. Marchant was at the front, racing toward them as if he were forty instead of seventy. Susannah was right behind him, her green dress floating around her trim legs.

"Please," the woman in his arms murmured again. She looked at him, the expression in her blue eyes lost and bewildered. He wondered if she might be on drugs. Hitting her head on the windshield might account for this unfocused, glazed look, but it couldn't explain the crazy driving.

"Please, put me down. Susannah... The wedding..."

Chase's arms tightened instinctively, and he froze in his tracks. She whimpered, and he realized he might be hurting her. "Say that again?"

"The wedding. I have to stop it."

* * * * *

Be sure to look for TEXAS BABY,
available September 11, 2007,
as well as other fantastic Superromance titles
available in September.

Welcome to Cowboy Country...

TEXAS BABY

by Kathleen O'Brien

#1441

Chase Clayton doesn't know what to think.
A beautiful stranger has just crashed his
engagement party, demanding that he not
marry because she's pregnant with his baby.
But the kicker is—he's never seen her before.

Look for TEXAS BABY and other fantastic
Superromance titles on sale September 2007.

Available wherever books are sold.

HARLEQUIN
Super Romance®

**Where life and love weave together
in emotional and unforgettable ways.**

nocturne™

KISS ME DEADLY

by

MICHELE HAUF

When vampire Nikolaus Drake swears
vengeance on the witch who almost killed
him, a misdirected love spell causes him
instead to fall in love with his enemy—
Ravin Crosse. Now as the spell courses
through him, Nikolaus must choose
between loyalty to his tribe and the
forbidden desires of his heart....

*Available September
wherever books are sold.*

SN61771

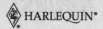

REQUEST YOUR FREE BOOKS!

2 FREE NOVELS PLUS 2 FREE GIFTS!

◆ HARLEQUIN®

INTRIGUE®

Breathtaking Romantic Suspense

YES! Please send me 2 FREE Harlequin Intrigue® novels and my 2 FREE gifts. After receiving them, if I don't wish to receive any more books, I can return the shipping statement marked "cancel." If I don't cancel, I will receive 6 brand-new novels every month and be billed just $4.24 per book in the U.S., or $4.99 per book in Canada, plus 25¢ shipping and handling per book and applicable taxes, if any*. That's a savings of close to 15% off the cover price! I understand that accepting the 2 free books and gifts places me under no obligation to buy anything. I can always return a shipment and cancel at any time. Even if I never buy another book from Harlequin, the two free books and gifts are mine to keep forever.

182 HDN EEZ7 382 HDN EEZK

Name	(PLEASE PRINT)	
Address		Apt. #
City	State/Prov.	Zip/Postal Code

Signature (if under 18, a parent or guardian must sign)

Mail to the **Harlequin Reader Service®:**
IN U.S.A.: P.O. Box 1867, Buffalo, NY 14240-1867
IN CANADA: P.O. Box 609, Fort Erie, Ontario L2A 5X3

Not valid to current Harlequin Intrigue subscribers.

Want to try two free books from another line?
Call 1-800-873-8635 or visit www.morefreebooks.com.

* Terms and prices subject to change without notice. NY residents add applicable sales tax. Canadian residents will be charged applicable provincial taxes and GST. This offer is limited to one order per household. All orders subject to approval. Credit or debit balances in a customer's account(s) may be offset by any other outstanding balance owed by or to the customer. Please allow 4 to 6 weeks for delivery.

Your Privacy: Harlequin is committed to protecting your privacy. Our Privacy Policy is available online at www.eHarlequin.com or upon request from the Reader Service. From time to time we make our lists of customers available to reputable firms who may have a product or service of interest to you. If you would prefer we not share your name and address, please check here. ☐

HI07

Bailey DelMonico has finally
gotten her life on track, and is
passionate about her recent career
change. Nothing will stand in the way
of her becoming a doctor...that is,
until she's paired with the sharp-tongued
Dr. Ivan Munro.

Watch the sparks fly in

Doctor in
the House

by *USA TODAY* Bestselling Author

Marie Ferrarella

Available September 2007

Intrigued? Read more at
TheNextNovel.com

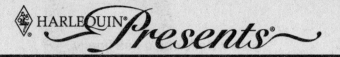

HARLEQUIN®

Mediterranean
N I G H T S™

*Experience glamour, elegance, mystery and revenge
aboard the high seas....*

Coming in September 2007...

BREAKING ALL
THE RULES

by

Marisa Carroll

Aboard the cruise ship *Alexandra's Dream* for
some R & R, sports journalist Lola Sandler is
surprised to spot pro-golfer Eric Lashman.
Years after walking away from the pro circuit
with no explanation to the public, Eric now
finds himself teaching aboard a cruise ship.

Lola smells a career-making exposé...
but their developing relationship may
force her to make a difficult choice.

www.eHarlequin.com   HM38963

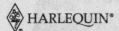

HARLEQUIN®

INTRIGUE®

COMING NEXT MONTH

#1011 RESTLESS WIND by Aimée Thurlo
Brotherhood of Warriors
Entrusted with the secrets of the Brotherhood of Warriors,
Dana Seles must aid Ranger Blueeyes to prevent the secret Navajo
order from extinction.

#1012 MEET ME AT MIDNIGHT by Jessica Andersen
Lights Out (Book 4 of 4)
On what was to be their first date, Secret Service agent Ty Jones
and Gabriella Solano have only hours to rescue the kidnapped vice
president.

#1013 INTIMATE DETAILS by Dana Marton
Mission: Redemption
On a mission to recover stolen WMDs, Gina Torno is caught by
Cal Spencer. Do they have conflicting orders or is each just playing
hard to get?

#1014 BLOWN AWAY by Elle James
After an American embassy bombing, T. J. Barton thought new love
Sean McNeal died in the explosion. But when he reappears, T.J. and
Sean must shadow the country's most powerful citizens in order to
stop a high-class conspiracy.

#1015 NINE-MONTH PROTECTOR by Julie Miller
The Precinct: Vice Squad
After Sarah Cartwright witnesses a mob murder, it's up to Detective
Cooper Bellamy to protect her—and her unborn child. But has he
crossed the line in falling for his best friend's sister?

#1016 BODYGUARD CONFESSIONS by Donna Young
When the royal palace of Taer is attacked, Quamar Bazan Al Asadi
begins a desperate race across the Sahara with presidential daughter
Anna Cambridge and a five-month-old royal heir. Can they restore
order before the rebels close in?

www.eHarlequin.com

HICNM0807